Just Is Not Enough

Haleigh Falcon

HALEIGH FALCON

Cover and Edge Design by Daqri Designs

Editing and Proofreading by Haleigh Falcon and Jessica A.M. (@jessica.am.author)

Printed in the USA by 48 Hour Books and Kindle Direct Publishing

Contents

Dedication

If you don't like the words cock, fuck, and hole, just close the book now. This isn't for you.
If you don't like not-so-quiet dirty talking in public, this isn't for you.
If you don't like getting caught sexting your boyfriend, this isn't for you.
For the rest of you who stuck around...
Good Boy.

Content Warnings

The warnings below will give away spoilers. I will confirm there is no sexual assault or mentioning of sexual assault of any kind anywhere in this book. However, there is physical assault in a non-sexual manner. If you know you do not have any triggers, proceed at your own discretion. If you have any other concerns regarding triggering content, please continue below. Your mental health and well-being is of the utmost importance and means more to me than reading my story!

Spoilers Below

This book may contain some triggering topics such as homophobic phrases (mentioned from past experiences), non-demonstrative family unit, aggressive/violent physical behavior against an MMC (non-sexual), and unbeknownst stalking.

Spotify Playlist

The following songs were part of my process in creating Kaden and Luke's story. I included chapter numbers in suggested order for you to listen along with the chapters that inspired each song. If you choose to, I hope you enjoy the songs while reading about my guys as much as I did while creating them. <3

<u>Just Is Not Enough by Haleigh Falcon Playlist</u>

Ch.1...........Nothing Else Matters by Alien Cake

Ch. 2...........Would? by Alien Cake

Ch. 3...........Work It by Missy Elliot

Ch. 3...........STAY by The Kid Laroi ft. Justin Beiber

Ch. 5...........embarrassing by Taylor Bickett

Ch. 7...........Seduction by BenzMuzik

Ch. 8...........Rush by Troye Sivan

Ch. 10.........Obsessed by Mariah Carey

Ch. 11.........Make You Feel My Love by Adele

Introduction

Kaden

I'm a little anxious—I'm aware of this fact. I've done my best to maneuver through life with minimal effects from it. Although, it does make it hard to meet guys. My track record hasn't been the greatest in the relationship department. I stopped believing in love and soulmates, no matter how many times my sister tried to convince me Mr. Right was out there. Then one night, one party, changed it all. There's only one problem—he's straight. Just my luck. He's off limits...until he's not.

Luke

No relationships, and stay focused on my goals. That was the plan. It had worked for years...until he came along. Kaden is the most adorable and alluring person I've ever met. Everything about him draws me into his orbit. I've never been attracted to a man before, but I can't resist him. After one night turns into something much more than I ever expected, there isn't anything I wouldn't do for him. His happiness is of the utmost importance to me, until protecting him takes precedence.

Author's Note

There is a character in this series whose name is taken from something created after he was born. Elder Emos, please don't question or criticize me for it yet. If you enjoy Luke and Kaden's story and decide to continue with the series, book two will explain everything! I promise to stomp on your heart a little, too, while explaining. <3

Chapter One

ANXIETY IS MY MIDDLE NAME

Kaden

"Will you just stop complaining and get ready," Lanie scolds me.

Siblings can be annoying—or really pushy in Lanie's case. She's always forcing me to step out of my comfort zone, even though she means well. Lanie is the best little sister I could have asked for, and also my best friend.

"I am ready. I can still protest until we walk in that door. It's our payment for dragging me to this thing. Deal with it."

She knows me better than anyone, sometimes more than I know myself. Lanie knows I don't like being in big crowds. The thought alone makes me anxious. Peopling is not my thing. I get to do enough of that at work. Dealing with people in my personal time is limited to my inner circle as much as possible.

Being a dentist, I'm with people all day. One-on-one is easier, though, and they usually have my hands in their mouths. At least there, I don't have to talk about myself. I can mindlessly make small talk about their dental hygiene and the weather, if necessary.

Meeting new people, in a casual setting? I get all in my head and forget to listen to the conversation. Ask me their name a minute after they told me, and I will have no clue. I've convinced myself I can't be the only person like this.

Lucky me to have a sister who happens to be the most outgoing person I have ever met. The social butterfly at every event. She knows when I zone out and saves me every time by taking the attention off me and onto her in some way. One time she even jumped on the nearest bar stool, dancing and making a spectacle of herself. We are different in many ways but so in tune with each other at the same time. She's the type of fun I want to be.

Mom always said, "I made sure to put some extra spice in Lanie's DNA to keep us on our toes, since you were such an easy baby. I may have put too much."

That's me, always 'the easy child.' The quiet, straight-A student who never made my parents worry about a thing. My sister being the wild one gave them enough worries for both of us. I'd added what I'd thought was first worry to the list by coming out senior year of high school.

To say they were not surprised would be an understatement. After working myself up with courage, I had run into the living room and blurted out, "I'm gay" with my eyes shut. I'd held my breath for a few moments, trying not to let the anxiety build up, waiting to hear their reaction.

It wasn't that I thought my parents would be the kind of people to disown their child for being gay—far from it. My parents are two of the coolest people around, but I'd worried about adding more stress to their plate, knowing how queer people were treated in our society at the time. Shit, it's still not much better now.

When I had finally opened my eyes, Dad had said, "Was that supposed to be a secret? Do I need to act surprised?" looking to my mother for the right answer.

Ignoring my father, Mom had walked over to hug me. "Kaden, honey, I am so glad you worked up the courage to say it out loud. I knew you would get there on your own. I'm proud of you, baby." Always the nurturer. Anyone who knows her never wonders why she became a nurse.

I'd loved my parents even more for making it so easy. At the time, Lanie was the only person who *I thought* knew. I guess I'm worse at hiding things than I thought.

Not that I am ashamed of being gay in any way, but teenagers can be the worst. Growing up in a southern state didn't help either. Some southerners' mentality about queer people can be worse than others. Maybe not so much in the bigger cities, but in the rural areas, you see it more often. Hearing 'you're so gay' as an insult when someone did some dumb shit was practically a daily occurrence walking through the halls at school.

Waiting until graduation to come out was my personal preference. Starting college as an out, gay man, represented a 'new me' of sorts. It was slow going at first—trying to meet new people always stressed me out. I joined the LGBTQ+ club the second week of the first semester, which was a big step in and of itself. Everyone was very welcoming and sensitive with my social anxiety. I wouldn't say it was smooth sailing from there, but I had a lot of support. Having my best friends since middle school attending the same college was helpful, too. We all had different majors but tried to take any classes we had in common together if we could. Ender is far less social than I am, but Connor makes up for the both of us.

When I graduated dental school and started working at my Aunt Olivia's practice, I emerged as a somewhat confident gay man. Well, not exactly at first, but that's a story for another time.

I have no issues meeting guys to hook up with or get my dick sucked. There are plenty of apps or clubs that I can go to get a quick fix anytime I want. Dating men long-term is a completely different story. You're not likely to meet someone wanting a monogamous long-term commitment with either of those options. They're full of fuckboys.

Either way, no one has ever given me those sparks or butterflies everyone talks about. I honestly don't believe in them at this point. Lanie, on the other hand, does, so she insists on dragging me to every social event she can in the hopes of finding me 'Mr. Right.' I don't bother protesting anymore. If I do, she gets even feistier than her normal self.

Which leads me to my current situation. The Singles Jingle Bell Mingle party some local radio station is throwing the weekend before Christmas. The ever-optimistic, hopeless romantic in Lanie swears it's going to be the place we meet our forevers. She swears it will rub off on me one of these days.

She insists the only reason we haven't met our lobsters yet—my sister and her *Friends* addiction—is because whenever we go out, people always assume we're a couple and avoid us. We're always laughing and having so much fun together that I guess it looks like we're 'together.' It's weird when people make that mistake. Tonight, she says she has the solution to that little problem. I can't say I'm not terrified to see what she comes up with.

Chapter Two

I FOLLOWED MY OWN PATH

Luke

Why is my family so interested in my love life? Does everyone think I need to settle down by the time I turn thirty in a couple months, or will a catastrophe occur? Like the world would end if I don't get married and have kids as soon as possible. "Find a wife and have babies. I want to be a grandma while I can still have fun with them," Mom says on repeat every time I see her. It sounds weird coming from her. They wonder why I don't visit more often.

Jackson is all about finding a wife, and having two-point-five kids and a big house with a white picket fence. Don't get me wrong, I love my younger brother. He means more to me than anyone in this world. But I'm the 'rebellious bachelor' son who only visits a few times a year, even though I live less than an hour away. My brother and I may think differently about relationships, but we're more alike than we'd ever admit.

While he appeases my mother with her constantly sticking her nose in our personal lives, I hear, "Are you dating?" and "I can introduce you to that nice girl at the church, you know-Lucy's daughter. Didn't you go to middle school with her?" far more often from my mother's meddling. Sometimes the pressure gets to be too much to bother engaging in any conversations with her. It doesn't help that my parents act like we had the perfect childhood.

The tiny town outside Lancaster that I called home, where my parents still live, felt smaller than a shoebox to me. Getting out and moving to Charlotte was the best thing I could have done on my eighteenth birthday. I moved in with my mother's hippie sister, Aunt Brenda, and her wife Grace. Working in their café in NoDa those first few years laid the foundation for where my career is today.

I always knew I didn't want to be a police officer like most of my family were, going back generations. I was more at home in the kitchen than anywhere else growing up. I learned basic cooking skills from my Aunt Brenda, but watching as many cooking shows as I could helped a lot, too. I was creating my own recipes around the time I entered high school. After a couple years, my dishes were always a success at the dinner table.

Food is a form of art. Feeding people is my love language. The only thing I want to do is create food that people will talk about. Nothing makes me happier than seeing people enjoy my dishes. Showing my parents-I can be successful doing something I love, rather than following the family's footsteps into the academy, will be a bonus. It's like they bred us to be clones of them. When I didn't fit in that box, I was labeled the rebellious one.

Despite the disappointment that I was with my parents, I worked my way up in the city's restaurants over the past twelve years. I fine-tuned my chef's skills and learned the business side of running a restaurant from Brenda and Grace, along with friends I've made in the industry over the years. Taking those hospitality management classes at UNC helped me prepare to be a proper leader for my employees.

In less than three months, we open the doors to our first restaurant, Stonewood's Steakhouse, in the heart of the city. The hippie aunts o-ffered to invest half their savings and be silent partners, and my best friend, Gabe, is joining us in this three-way partnership, helping me fulfill this dream of mine. Getting a small business loan to cover the rest of the startup costs sealed the deal. I have been so focused on all things encompassing building a restaurant, I barely remember my name these days

.

Tonight's dilemma is my own fault. I agreed to go out with Jackson and our cousin, Dakota. They moved to the city about four years after I did, when they finished the academy together—the "good boys" who followed the family path set for them. If the family only knew what they got up to these days.

They're always trying to lure me out to sports bars with them. "Luke, this place has the best wings. You should come check them out," was one of their tactics last month, trying to appeal to the food lover in me. Those fuckers will find any excuse to get me to drink and pickup women with them.

As for tonight's excuse, Jackson said he needed me to be his wingman at a party Dakota heard about on some radio station. Apparently, Dakota is acting weird lately and hasn't been the best wingman after having a few beers. It's a lousy excuse since we're both blessed with Stonewood genes, giving us a sharp jawline, jade-green eyes that are accentuated by our raven hair, and a towering 6'3" that often attracts women all on its own. I'm not trying to be cocky, but neither of us have ever needed a wingman to pick up women. When I called him out on his shit, he 'fessed up, calling me a grump because I've been working too hard, and he thinks I need to get laid. Well, he's not wrong about that.

The problem is, fucking random women may be fun in the moment, but then what? Date? Get married? I barely stick around long enough for them to find their bras on the floor. I always let them know beforehand what to expect. I'm not out here trying to be that asshole women complain about to their friends. I have enough respect for women to not lead them on.

I don't need to get distracted by a relationship right now. My restaurant is my relationship and making it a success is all I care about. Dating would take my focus away from that, and I can't let that happen. I'm fine with my right hand in between going out to find the occasional hook-up.

He thinks he's slick, but I know Jackson is trying to please our mother by helping me find her a potential daughter-in-law. He thinks I'm lonely as much as she does.

So here I am, letting these two idiots convince me to go to some singles' meetup with them, hoping I meet the 'woman of my dreams.' I'll just settle for someone to replace my hand for the night.

Chapter Three

My Lively Sister Led Me to Him

Kaden

"Tell me again why I let you convince me to come tonight?" I sigh heavily at Lanie.

"Because you love me and know we'll have a good time, even if you insist you're not here to find your lobster." She thinks if she says it enough it will come true.

Faith, Lanie's favorite human aside from me, giggles as if finding my soulmate hasn't been *their* focus for the past couple of months. I swear they have a bet going to see how long it will take or something.

"Did you really need to wear that shirt?" I ask again, while we wait in line to get into the building. The party is being held in this big nightclub in the city. Waiting in line this long makes my legs feel like I'm on my morning run.

"Listen, if I don't tell all the men here that you're my brother, neither of us will be kissing any of them by the end of the night. It's easier this way." Lanie says, twirling around like a ballerina in her one-shoulder top and flowing mini skirt, acting like it's not 40º outside. How is she not freezing?

She knows I'll be glued to her side, as usual, so making a shirt that says 'He's Just My Brother, You Can Hit on Us' will get us some laughs at the least. She's so carefree, not giving a damn what people think of her. I want to be her when I grow up.

When we get to the admission counter, we're asked for our name, age, occupation, and sexual orientation. Apparently, our information goes on a digital list that's put in kiosks stationed around the bars where we can look each other up with numbers from our name tags. I feel like I'm at Sheetz ordering some road trip munchies. Who the hell comes up with this shit?

Once we're inside, Lanie and Faith make a beeline to the bar for drinks. I follow suit, knowing that having a few drinks is the only way I'll survive this night. There's already what feels like a hundred people here, which is about ninety-five strangers more than I can manage at once.

The club is a huge room with high ceilings and a big dance floor in the middle. On either side of the dance floor are two long bars with at least three bartenders working each. In the back of the room are a little more than a dozen high-top tables on a raised platform overlooking the dance floor.

"I'm ordering shots!" Lanie decides for all of us, like we could argue with her if we tried. For a 5'3", vertically challenged girl with light-blue eyes and mousy brown hair, you would think she'd be less bossy. At twenty-five years old, she can persuade me to do almost anything, despite me being three years older.

Lanie, of course, picks Tequila because why not? We do the Tequila ritual: salt on the one hand holding the lime, shot glass in the other. "To a night of laughing, dancing, and maybe a little smashing," she yells as we clink our shot glasses before licking the salt, downing the fiery liquid from hell, and shoving the lime in our mouths. I don't have time to recover from the fire ignited in my throat before she's ordering another round, but this time she asks the bartender to make them doubles for each of us. I don't know whether to be happy to let loose and have fun tonight, or dread the hangover I'll have tomorrow.

Thankfully, after the second round, Faith pulls us both out onto the dance floor. I'm not the best dancer, but I can hold my own, and at least I can get lost in the crowd where no one is paying attention.

The three of us must be a sight to see, dancing like we don't have a care in the world. The music is a perfect mix of songs from the early 2000s to current hits. One minute we're putting our thangs down and reversing it with Missy Elliott, the next we're jumping around to 'Stay' by The Kid Laroi.

It's much easier when I can pretend it's only us and the music. Until Lanie throws her head back and screeches, "Bathrooooooom!" at the top of her lungs. We all head to the restrooms, Faith and Lanie holding hands through the crowd to not lose each other. There's no line when they get to the ladies' room, and I continue farther down the hall to the men's room, glad to see no line here either. Walking in, I'm surprised to see the long line of both urinals and stalls. No wonder we didn't have to wait.

I finish breaking the seal and wash my hands quickly, hoping I didn't miss Lanie and Faith leaving the ladies' room. The last thing I want to do is wander around searching for them by myself.

Of course, I make it out there faster than them. I swear women have their own parties in the bathroom with how long they spend in there. I wait for a few minutes, until they come barreling out the door, laughing and ready to head back to the bar.

We only get halfway there when Lanie spots someone and does a double-take. Stopping next to a group of three guys, she leans in close to one of the taller ones with neatly styled jet-black hair, a chiseled jaw, and the goofiest smile on his face, waiting to see what she is doing. She mouths the four-digit number on his name tag as if committing it to memory, looks up to smile at him, and saunters away like she was lazily browsing at the grocery store. The confidence that oozes out of her is inspiring.

Instead of following her to the bar right away, I take a quick glance at the other two guys. The shorter one of the three is about my height at 6' tall. He's average-looking, but still attractive, though he has a strange look on his face as he watches my sister and Faith walk away. The third guy is nearly identical to Lanie's eye-catcher, except his hair is shaved on the sides but the top hangs low enough to make you want to reach up and sweep it away from those eyes that feel like they're burning right through my own. I break the stare first to avoid looking like a creeper.

Dear Goddesses, please let him be queer.

Chapter Four

MY FIRST IMPRESSION OF HIM

Luke

"Who was that little minx?" Jackson practically whispers, his wide eyes staring at the trio walking towards the bar on the far side of the room. I don't think I've ever seen someone with cartoon heart eyes, until now.

"Her number is 2759," Dakota blurts out and smiles, proud of himself. "I glanced at it while she was eyeing you up." Being four beers deep, I'm surprised he had the wherewithal to think fast enough to look at her tag.

My brother sets forth on his mission to find a kiosk at the closest bar, typing her number in to pull up their group. The event planners arranged the list to display all members of a group when entering any of their numbers in.

"Lanie, twenty-five years old, and she's a nurse," Jackson mumbles, barely loud enough to hear over the music.

I look over his shoulder to see the rest of the group. Faith, twenty-six years old, hairstylist. The fiery, red hair fits her perfectly.

Last on the list, Kaden, twenty-eight years old, dentist. That explains the nerdy doctor type vibe I got from him even in casual clothes. He lingered back with us after Lanie and Faith walked away. The piercing stare he had on me sucked all of the air from the room. I had to cover up the search for oxygen my lungs ached for by pretending to take a sip of my beer. Those eyes were captivating. I'm glad he broke eye contact first because I couldn't do it. I'm not gay—no doubt I like women—but I'm not embarrassed to admit he's a very attractive man. It's not the first time I've appreciated a man's appearance, but that was...intense.

He reminds me of the doctor Gabe told me he had a crush on when he was a teenager. When Gabe had mono in high school, his mom took him to an urgent care. He said the doctor was so gorgeous he purposely faked being sick so his mom would keep taking him back to see him. Gabe said that doctor was his first 'never could be mine' love and doctors aren't supposed to be that hot. I'm guessing Kaden is that kind of dentist for some teenagers.

I glance at the last column next to Kaden's name instead of following the guys to the bar next to the kiosk. 'Sexual Orientation: Gay.' Why does that make our encounter that much more interesting?

"Do you see her? I have to talk to her. What do I do?" Jackson's rapid-fire questions are in sync with his emotions, his eyes desperately scanning the room when we step over to the bar.

Big brother to the rescue. I get the bartender's attention to order him some liquid courage. "Can we get three shots of Tequila, please?" I forego passing around the salt and lime—we don't have time for that. One shot should be good enough, then we can go back to beer. I will not be held responsible for these guys vomiting at the end of the night.

"Be chill man, she's obviously interested. We can walk along the perimeter of the dance floor. I'm sure we'll find her," I say, handing him the shot glass.

Jackson downs his shot and leads the way, determination in his eyes. It takes us a few minutes to spot them on the dance floor. All three dancing together like they're in their own little bubble. My brother looks like he's about to hyperventilate. Geez, this must be what the hippie aunts meant by "love at first sight" when they told me how they met. I'm not a believer in the notion.

Jackson takes a step forward, then backward before turning to walk away, and then immediately about-facing to watch the trio again. Poor guy doesn't know what to do with himself. This should be fun.

"Dakota, I need you to distract the friend while I try to talk to her," Jackson begs, not taking his eyes off the girl now.

Dakota doesn't miss a beat. "On it. What about her brother?" Bad wingman, my ass.

"How do you know he's her brother?" I question, wondering where he got that information.

"It's right on her shirt. Am I the only one paying attention here?" Dakota sighs in frustration.

Not understanding, I walk around to Jackson's other side, squeezing between him and Dakota for a better view. The front of Lanie's shirt says, 'He's Just My Brother, You Can Hit on Us.' Is that supposed to be a joke? I don't get it.

"Well, with a shirt like that, I doubt he's the overprotective type who'll bite your head off for talking to her." I try to point out something positive.

"Once we start talking, I'm sure he'll get the hint and make himself scarce," Jackson says, nudging Dakota forward as they make their way to the dance floor.

I walk to the closest bar, taking a spot with a perfect view of the possible trainwreck about to occur. If the redhead winds up slapping Dakota, the night away from menu planning for the restaurant will be well worth it.

Approaching the trio, Dakota slides up behind the redhead, resting his hands on her hips. He leans down close to her ear and says something to her. She turns around slowly, with a glare that could burn through a glacier, shoving Dakota hard. She yells something at Lanie and Kaden over the music and motions that she's okay, then stalks off towards the bathroom by herself. Dakota heads off in the same direction probably to apologize for whatever asinine thing he said to her. Called it. He may be terrible at hitting on women, but he got the job Jackson gave him done.

Jackson is already by Lanie's side, leaning in to talk to her. They start laughing as Jackson joins in, dancing with both Lanie and her brother. Kaden turns to walk away when his sister grabs his hand and spins him back into them. All three continue dancing together, but damn, I'm feeling second-hand embarrassment. Kaden isn't a bad-looking guy or dancer. Why has he not found another guy to dance with by now? Ugh, guess I should be a good wingman and help my brother while also saving Kaden from this awkward situation. How did I get into this position again?

"Hey, 'Just the Brother,' why don't we go have a beer and let these two get to know each other?" I say, hanging my arm across his shoulders, pulling him back to the bar I came from.

Walking back to the bar, I don't remove my arm from his shoulders, and I'm not sure why. He smells good though. I'll have to remember to ask him what cologne he wears.

When we get to the bar, I make sure to position us where we can still see Lanie and Jackson. I don't want him to think we're a bunch of creeps trying to hurt his sister.

"What are you drinking?" I ask, waving down a bartender. I notice Kaden staring at me wide-eyed—I'm not sure if he's blinked since we left our siblings—and his jaw practically on the floor. Is he in shock?

"Hey, are you okay?" I finally get a blink from him but still no words. I can't stop myself from smiling. This is going to be *so* fucking fun. Jackson owes me big time for this one.

Chapter Five

Enrolled Class: Ways to Embarrass Yourself 101

Kaden

What the fuck is happening right now?

Breathe, Kaden.

It's not like I've never hung out with a straight guy before-obviously-but we're not going there. At least, I think he's straight. He's your standard, run-of-the-mill straight guy, no different from anyone else. He only happens to be the most stunning man I've ever been face-to-face with...and has the greenest eyes that bore into the depths of my soul...and perfect teeth surrounded by plump lips...and he's tall with a body most men dream of having...and those veins bulging through the tattoos on his forearms below his rolled-up sleeves of his black button-down shirt that molds to his body like it's been shrink wrapped onto him. Is it too soon to ask him to take it off?

Good grief, what's wrong with me? I think my brain is short-circuiting.

Kaden get ahold of yourself. He asked you a question-answer it!

"Uh, I'll take a whiskey, thanks." Did he offer to pay? I don't think he offered to pay. Why would he offer to pay? He doesn't know me.

What is wrong with you Kaden? Fix it!

"Here, I'll pay." Grabbing my card from my wallet, I shove it at his chest like a madman. Yep, the pecs are hard as steel. Goddesses-take the wheel, I'm going down in flames here.

"It's cool, I'll get the first round. Looks like we might be a while anyway." Mr. 'Just Here for the Beer' smirks, pushing my hand back toward me.

His fingers are warm around my wrist. I wonder how they would feel around my co...no sir, we are not going there!

He. Is. Straight!

We don't mess around with straight men Kaden.

I don't even know his name for crying out loud. When Lanie ran to the kiosk to find out who her mystery man was, I noticed my present company apparently wants to be here as little as I did. He listed his name as 'Just Here for the Beer.' Could he be any less cheeky?

The list also said he's twenty-nine years old, a 'business owner,' and under Sexual Orientation,' 'unknown.' That kind of sounds like a confused straight guy to me, which means off limits. Experimenting can get messy.

"Thanks, appreciate it." I fumble the card attempting to put it back in my wallet, sending it flying out of my hands and onto the floor. I turn to pick it up, and when I straighten up, I see him staring at my ass as he slides a whiskey glass at me.

"So, do I call you Kaden, or would you rather be 'Just the Brother' all night?"

Cheeky. "I'll be Kaden tonight, thanks. I mean, I'm Kaden every night, not just tonight. Well, days too. Since the day I was born. It's not like I go around changing my name between days and nights. Holy Goofy Goobers, can you stop me from speaking, or forget everything that came out of my mouth in the last twenty seconds, please?"

Nice Kaden. Real smooth.

Mr. I Still Don't Know His Name laughs at me. Loudly. Kill me now. "Kaden, you're funny. Was that a SpongeBob quote? I didn't know dentists could be funny. They're usually all scary with their drills and needles." He shudders, probably thinking of my everyday tools.

"Glad I can change your opinion of us scary dentists. Now you'll think of us as bumbling fools instead. What a step up." Shaking my head, I keep my eyes trained on my glass, hoping to regain some of my composure.

"It's a good step up," he says, popping my head up I catch him grinning.

"Do I get to know your name yet or should I call you 'Just Here for the Beer' guy all night?" I earn another hearty laugh from him, which gives me a tiny sliver of hope that I haven't fucked this up, yet.

"The name's Luke. Nice to formally meet you, Kaden." Great, he's holding his hand out for me to shake, like I'll be able to act human after touching him.

"Nice to meet you, Luke." His hand grips mine firmly. "So, what kind of business do you own?" I ask hoping to appear in control, while my thoughts are racing laps around my brain like they're Usain Bolt.

"Keeping notes on me, are you?" he says, flashing those pearly whites again.

Heat rushes to my face. "No!" I blurt out and take a deep breath. "At least you knew my name before you dragged me off the dance floor. It's hard not to notice how vague you are about yourself. What's so bad that you don't want people to know anything about you? Are you a criminal? Are you in hiding? Are you with the mafia? Oh wait, are you in witness protection?"

This would be a good time to stop talking, Kaden.

Chapter Six

I Like Learning Things About Him and Myself

Luke

I can't help but throw my head back, laughing at his rambling. "You're fascinating, Kaden. It's refreshing." I try to simmer down, not wanting to hurt his feelings by laughing at him.

I notice the way his eyes light up from my modest praise. He finally shows a hint of a smile behind all the nervousness, and his shoulders relax the slightest bit.

"No, I'm not in hiding or any of that. But if I were, would I tell you?" I say with a grin.

"Well, I suppose not. Then why all the secrecy?"

"I didn't want to be here. My brother and cousin think I need to get out more, said I work too much. They convinced me to come tonight against my better judgement. So, I'm here, but if someone wants to know something about me, they can ask me. I'm not a steak on a menu you can order without earning the right to eat it first. I don't give everyone and anyone access to me." That may have come off cocky, but he doesn't react.

I realize I said I *didn't* want to be here. Interesting.

"Asked and still not answered." Kaden gestures toward me with a hand and wide eyes, as if I forgot he had asked me already. I did.

He quickly follows up with, "or have I not earned access yet?" Surprisingly, he has.

"I am an owner by title, chef at heart. My first restaurant opens in three months." I subconsciously puff my chest out with pride.

"Someone is proud of himself," he says, acknowledging the movement. "Rightfully so, given the accomplishment at your age." He gives me a small smile, enough to reveal a dimple on his right cheek I hadn't noticed until now. Dimples are cute.

My cheeks heat with...embarrassment? No, that's not it.

"When you know what you want in life, you go after it. No matter what it takes," I say with determination.

"Yeah, I suppose we should," Kaden ponders, his gaze never leaving mine.

Is he blushing?

He exhales softly before turning away and redirecting the topic. "I feel like a piece of meat on a menu being on that list, too. I'm not used to being put on display. It's uncomfortable." His voice is calmer, less nervous than it was a few minutes ago.

"You don't seem uncomfortable now. What's different?"

He hesitates before answering. "Probably the whiskey," he says, shrugging one shoulder.

I follow his gaze turning to look over his shoulder at the dance floor. Jackson and Lanie are still laughing and dancing together, looking like they're enjoying each other's company.

"What's with the shirt, anyway? Is it a joke or something?" I ask, nodding toward Lanie.

"My sister's answer to making sure everyone knew we weren't a couple. For some reason, it happens more often than you'd think," Kaden muses.

"That's weird, but you two must be close if people are assuming that."

"Yeah, we were always close growing up. She's my best friend. I mean, look at her. She's a lot of fun to be around. How could you not love her?" he says with clear adoration.

"And you're not?" I raise an eyebrow, confused.

He turns back to face me. "Not what?"

"Not fun to be around," I clarify.

"I don't know. I guess I can be with my family and friends. Strangers, not so much."

"Well, I'm a stranger and I'm having fun with you." I flash him a coy smile.

Did that sound like I was flirting with him?

Why am I flirting with him?

Kaden is back to staring blankly at me.

I move the conversation to something completely different after that, mentioning the type of music the DJ is playing. That seems like a safe topic. We discover we both lean toward liking rock music, and even some heavy metal, more than any other genre. This turns into us both rattling off the bands we love, and our favorite songs from each album. I will neither confirm nor deny that we may have belted out the chorus of 'The Devil in I' by Slipknot. I'm not sure when last time I had this much fun, especially with talking to someone I hardly know.

We get lost in more conversation that flows effortlessly. Every once in a while, he glances toward his sister, obviously checking to make sure she's okay. Lanie and Jackson are lost in their own little world—it seems they've hit it off well. Nearby, Faith is dancing with Dakota.

Kaden is much more relaxed now. He hasn't even noticed his whiskey is gone. I flag down the bartender again. "You're empty, want another?" I gesture at his glass.

"Are you trying to get me drunk now, Luke?" Kaden counters, a coquettish grin in place.

That, I know, is flirting!

Those captivating eyes are now filled with something resembling desire. The way he says my name does things to me, and I can't explain why.

A sudden rush of warmth hits my face and the hairs on my arms tingle where they meet my skin. I like the feeling.

Not knowing how to answer his question, I look for the bartender and hurriedly order two double shots of Tequila, a beer, and a whiskey.

Lost for words, I slowly pull out my wallet to get my credit card, stalling for time until the bartender comes back with our drinks.

"Let me get this round." Kaden hands me his card with one hand while his other hand wraps around my forearm.

It momentarily stuns me. I stare down at my arm, relishing the feeling of his strong hand and warm skin against mine.

Well, that sure feels different. In a good way.

Kaden must see me staring, because he jerks his hand back to his side. "Sorry, I didn't mean to offend you," he blurts out.

I immediately miss the warmth of his hand on my skin. I slowly raise my head, the hazy feeling fading.

"You didn't offend me, Kaden. At all," I tell him, my tone firm, and gaze fixed on him.

The dimple is back again. "Good," he replies, not taking his eyes off me as he hands his card to the bartender who's watched this all unfold. The smug asshole walks away, card in hand, with a knowing smirk.

I'm not entirely sure what's happening here, but I don't want it to stop. Kaden is a great guy, and funny, too. It's obvious he has a different effect on me than any man has before. Hell, no woman has even had this kind of effect on me. I've never been attracted to men more than thinking they were objectively good-looking or had a nice physique. What's different about him from the others? This doesn't make me bi, does it? That doesn't make sense. I'm an ally, but I've never considered myself queer in any way. I hadn't been given a reason to, until now.

Am I willing to explore this? With Kaden?

I slam my shot back and chase it with my beer. I regret it immediately when the mix of flavors linger on my taste buds.

"How did you become a dentist at such a young age? Don't you have to go to school for a billion years or some shit?" I try changing the subject and wind up staring at him like it's for the first time.

Kaden goes on to tell me about taking college courses while still in high school and that helped fast track the path to his degrees.

I start getting lost, admiring his strong jawline, sky-blue eyes, full lips, and the way his slightly curly hair hangs long enough to curtain his face, the chocolate-brown shade making his eyes pop even more. I imagine he has a baby face without the day-old scruff, but it suits him well. I can tell by the snug fit of his gray chinos and black polo that he takes care of his body.

Blood rushes straight to my cock. Kaden is *very* different from other men. My brain knew this, and now my cock has finally caught up to the fact.

"Luke, you okay?" Kaden asks with concern, noticing me spacing out I suppose. I don't know how long I was gone.

"Uhm, sorry. Yeah, I'm okay. I think I might be feeling the alcohol." I let out a nervous laugh at my lie.

Man, what an interesting turn of events. This is the last thing I expected would happen tonight. Maybe skipping the menu planning wasn't such a bad thing after all.

Chapter Seven

I Proposition Him

Kaden

Luke just had the strangest look on his face. At first, it almost looked like he was checking me out with the way his eyes touched every inch of my face and then roamed down my body. He even licked his lips at one point.

Can you be jealous of lips?

Then his expression had turned to, I don't know, shock? Annoyance? I know I'm not magazine cover-worthy, but I don't think I look that bad tonight.

"Do you need to sit down or something? Some water?" I wave to the bartender.

"Water might be good. Maybe I had one too many beers." Luke swipes his forehead and sighs.

One too many beers? He's a big guy—I'm sure he can handle his alcohol. He seemed fine all night. Maybe he's looking for an excuse to ditch me.

"If you want to go find your cousin, I won't be offended. You don't need to keep me company." I don't need someone pitying me for being a third wheel. Here I thought we were having a good conversation.

My anxiety takes hold of me quickly. I don't bother waiting for a response and start to walk away. I don't get to take my second step, though. Luke stopping me with his hand on my bicep.

I turn and am struck by the longing look on his face, his eyes pleading with me. "I don't want to find anyone else. I *want* to be right here with you. Stay, please," he says, letting go of my arm.

The tsunami of butterflies in my stomach takes flight, attempting to escape. Well, look at that—he's made a believer out of me.

"I'm sorry if I'm acting weird. I was...I'm..." He bites his lower lip, stopping himself from saying anything further.

Where did the cheeky, peacock of a man I was with earlier tonight go? The look in his eyes right now is confusing the fuck out of me. Why does he seem nervous now?

"Luke, what is going on? One minute we're having a good conversation, and the next, you're acting all weird. Did I say something wrong?"

"No. You didn't say anything wrong. I don't know. I've never met anyone like you, Kaden." Luke's eyes dart away briefly, and then back to me.

"What, gay? Didn't peg you for a bigot." I let out a scoff. What the hell is up with this guy?

The fucker laughs at me. "No, Kaden. Do I really look like a bigot to you? I only meant you're...different, in a good way. An unexpected way." The confidence is back in his voice, along with a hungry gaze aimed right at me.

This guy is hurting my neck from all this whiplash.

"If I'm being truly honest here, I don't normally find myself appreciating another man's physique. At least not in the way it makes my dick hard," Luke says, maintaining eye contact, waiting to get confirmation that I understand exactly what he said.

And we have lift off! He has my dick's full and undivided attention. I did not expect that much honesty, but I'm not hating it, either.

"You have my attention." I see the moment he notices the craving in my eyes. "And what do you plan on doing about your...situation?" My eyes slowly move down to the bulge in his pants. My ass is suddenly jealous of a pair of slacks, wanting his cock inside me instead.

He notices where my eyes have wandered to. "I haven't quite figured that part out yet, but I'm open to suggestions." He throws me a wink followed by a mischievous grin.

My cheeky peacock is back.

He's not yours Kaden!

He can be mine for tonight!

The slightly inebriated side of my brain internally yells at the logical side of my brain to shut that bitch up.

I look at the dance floor where Lanie and Jackson are still together. She seems like she's in good hands, and Faith is nearby, surprisingly dancing with Dakota.

I turn back towards Luke, his face amused with questioning eyes.

He's straight—this could get messy. We don't do messy.

He's merely experimenting.

It'll be a one and done. I can keep this un-messy. I know I can.

It's not worth the risk. Never again.

While I go back to arguing with that logical bitch, Luke indiscreetly adjusts himself, letting his hand linger briefly to make sure I take notice.

Fuck it, that's a future me problem. He's too mouthwatering to pass up tasting him, just once. I'll save regret for tomorrow.

I lean into him with my lips pressed gently against his ear, speaking barely loud enough for him to hear me over the music. "I'm going to the restroom now. I suggest you meet me in the farthest stall from the door so we can take care of this little problem of yours." I gently suck in his earlobe before pulling away, lightly grazing the back of my hand against his dick print as I turn away from him. I swear I hear him gasp. As I head toward the restroom, I force myself not to look back.

JUST IS NOT ENOUGH

Please, Goddesses, make him follow me!

Chapter Eight

I Discover Two Fun Facts About Myself

Luke

Whoa, confident Kaden has entered the building, and why is it so fucking hot? I thought my cock was hard admiring his body, but with the combination of his proposition and his gentle touch, it's now solid titanium.

Prior to tonight, my first thought wouldn't have been to follow Kaden to the men's room. Spending the last few hours with him has made me think otherwise, though. I not only enjoyed his company—I'm extremely fucking turned on by him. There's no way I can stop myself from going after him.

The thought alone of him wrapping those plump lips around my cock has me wanting to run full speed in his direction to let it happen.

Instead, I wait a couple minutes to make sure he's able to get a stall, even if my heart is pounding inside my chest like it's trying to break out and my cock is throbbing in sync with it to the point it's almost painful.

I calm my breathing and finish my beer in one swig. Feeling confident I waited long enough, I stride toward the men's room, avoiding eye contact with everyone in my path. I don't need any distractions slowing me down from getting to what's waiting for me in that stall.

When I walk into the long galley-style restroom, there are only a handful of guys scattered between the urinals and sinks. I go to the farthest stall at the end of the room, attempting to act casual.

Then I slowly push against the door.

It opens, revealing Kaden sitting on the tank portion of the toilet, elbows on his knees with his feet on the seat. His lust-filled eyes lock on mine. I take a quick glance back toward the rest of the room, then walk into the stall, turning the lock behind me.

Instantly, Kaden's feet are on the ground as he grabs hold of me. He turns me, slamming my back to the wall, with his body crashing into me and covering my mouth with his palm.

"I'm going to need you to cover your mouth with your fist while I take care of this," Kaden whispers in my ear, palming the outline of my cock, squeezing way more softly than it's needing to be touched right now. "I suggest you keep it there, or we'll have an audience hearing you make the lewdest sounds from me deep-throating your cock until I have your eyes rolling back in your head and your knees giving out, making you come so hard someone will have to help you remember what your name is when I'm done." Humiliatingly enough, I can't hold back another gasp from under his hand.

He pulls back, his one hand leaving my mouth and joining the other, now under my shirt at my waistband. Kaden pauses, looking me in the eyes as if waiting for my permission. I give him the nod he seems to be silently asking for, while I raise my fist to my mouth and close my teeth around a couple knuckles.

"Good boy."

My eyes flutter as I cast my hungry gaze downward. His indecently peering eyes accompanied by a wicked grin. He clearly enjoyed hearing my soft groan from his praise.

Huh, who knew I liked being praised?

Kaden leans his face into the crook of my neck, inhaling deeply as he undoes my button and zipper. My head lolls back against the wall and I breathe deeply through my nose.

Teeth latch on to my Adam's apple, biting roughly, followed by a flat tongue slowly licking over the wounded area.

He pulls my slacks and boxer briefs down to my thighs in one swift tug, leaving my cock out at full mast for him. His hand wraps firmly around my length, thumb swiping away the pre-cum already forming on my tip.

Kaden nips my neck once more before sliding down on his haunches, taking a good look at what I have to offer. My gaze falls to enjoy the view of him on his knees for me.

"Impressive," he says, looking up at me with raised eyebrows.

I don't have time to respond when he suddenly flattens his tongue over my balls, sucking one after the other into his mouth while languidly stroking my cock. He makes sure to give equal attention to each one, then begins to lick his way up my shaft from base to head. The tip of his tongue presses firmly into the slit, causing my body to tremble uncontrollably.

His seductive eyes are fixed on mine as he engulfs my dick, one palm against my ass, pushing me deeper until the head hits the back of his throat.

My teeth clamp down on my fist attempting to hold back the animalistic grunt I make when he swallows around the tip. He doesn't even gag. His fingers tighten around my ass, and he gives a slight head shake. The sensations make my stomach tighten and my nostrils flare, staring down at the sinful sight, silently pleading for more. His brows arch, his lips still tightly wrapped around my shaft, giving me a warning not to make a sound. I nod in compliance.

Kaden slides back up my length, hollowing his cheeks. The suction is strong enough to make my hips buck as I chase the feeling.

Taking hold of my free hand, he places it on the back of his head, squeezing my fingers, clenching a patch of his curls up in them. The hand on my ass pushes my body further against his face while the other covering my hand pushes his head forward, letting me know exactly what he expects of me.

Say no more, Kaden.

Not wasting another moment, I tighten my hold on his hair and thrust forward with full force. I pause for the briefest moment to check on him. When I see Kaden's eyes turn black with lust, it sends me into a frenzy. The sheer force I start fucking his mouth with, immediately brings tears to his eyes.

Kaden is holding onto the back of my thighs for dear life as I continue hammering my cock into his throat, not letting up for a second. He's unleashed something feral in me that I didn't realize was there. Keeping my fist in my mouth, knowing I couldn't stay quiet if I tried, I clench my teeth tighter around it.

Admit it, Luke, you're keeping it there to please him by being his Good Boy.

Why does that thought make my knees weak? I'm thankful for the music outside the room covering up our heavy breathing and the indecent sound Kaden's mouth around my cock is making, so we don't have the audience he warned me about.

The sight of snot beginning to drip out his nose, tears streaming down his pink cheeks, and his hooded eyes conveying how much he's enjoying himself, is obscene and beautiful at the same time, sending me over the edge.

My balls draw up tighter when I halt thrusting with them pressed against his chin, my cum shooting directly down his throat. I'm seeing stars behind my clenched eyelids. He easily swallows every drop as my cock pulses until it's emptied all I have to give him.

What the fuck was that? I've never been that rough when getting head from a woman. I'm too afraid to hurt them. Kaden welcomed it wholeheartedly and I won't complain, having come so hard I have to grip his shoulders to regain my balance.

Kaden rises to his full height, smiling like the Cheshire Cat, wiping his face with the back of his hands. "Such a good boy," he acknowledges my accomplishment. My smile mirrors his at the approval.

Feeling sated, I instinctively go to pull him in close by the nape of his neck to kiss him, when he pulls back, pushing his palms against my chest.

Why does that make my stomach twist uncomfortably?

Chapter Nine

THEY BOTH SCARE ME

Kaden

The expression on Luke's face when I stopped him from kissing me tells me I did the right thing. I've seen it on someone in the past. It's the look a straight man gets when he's satisfied with everything we did together, but once the high wears off, the not knowing how he feels about it inevitably comes.

A.k.a messy!

As fun as this night has been, I can't do this again. I swore off straight men after He Who Shall Not Be Mentioned. No one is worth that kind of pain again. No matter how phenomenal his cock felt down my throat, taking this any further than that, may ruin me this time around.

"Uh, sorry. That was fun, though," I sputter out, not knowing how to keep this from being more awkward than it has suddenly become.

"I can have my cock down your throat, but I can't kiss you?" Thankfully, the music pumping in the background is louder than his statement.

His facial expression has changed to indignation, complete with furrowed brows and tight lips. Is he hurt? I don't know how to explain without sounding like an asshole. Luke is a nice guy. I don't want to hurt his feelings.

"You're straight, Luke. I'm fully aware. We had a good time. Let's leave it at that."

"I'm not saying I want to marry you after one blowjob, Kaden. I don't see how one kiss would change that. And I think it's a little obvious after my reaction to your company tonight and all this"—he motions between me and his now half-flaccid dick, pants still around his thighs—"that I might be a little less straight than I was yesterday." Luke sounds like that logical bitch in my head now.

Attempting to avoid giving a response, I turn to unlock the stall door to leave when Luke stops me.

With his hand on the door holding it closed, Luke softly whispers in my ear, "I'm not done with you yet, Kaden." His hand falls, briefly caressing mine on the door lock before dropping to his side. My forearms are littered with goosebumps.

I take one last glance over my shoulder, expecting to see the same hurt expression from minutes ago. Instead, I see tenacity. He means what he said.

Without saying another word, I walk out of the stall.

Leaving the restroom, I quickly search for Lanie and Faith. I find them with Jackson and Dakota, near one of the bars. I attempt to ignore the pain in my scalp from how tight a grasp Luke had on my hair.

"Hey, there you are! I was looking for you. We were about to send Dakota to hunt you down in the bathroom." Lanie's initial playful expression turns to concern when she looks closely at my face.

"Yeah, I wasn't feeling well. I think I had too much to drink. I think I want to head out—it's getting late anyway." I add the last part when I see Luke approaching.

"Okay, yeah. Let's get going." Lanie's voice sounds strained. I know she's worried about me now, and I hate it.

She says goodbye to Jackson while handing him her phone, exchanging numbers.

Faith and Dakota give each other awkward looks when she walks away to join me and whispers, "You alright, Kaden?"

I nod my response, avoiding the temptation to glance in Luke's direction while we give the casual 'see you around' wave goodbye. Turning to walk away, I can't stop myself from getting one last look at Luke.

I instantly regret it. Luke's determined gaze is aimed right at me, chin turned upward in confidence.

This man is going to be trouble, I can feel it.

Messy.

"What the fuck happened in there?" Lanie demands as soon as we hit the pavement to wait for our Uber to show up.

"Nothing, why? I got sick in the bathroom." She doesn't need to know the sordid details of my little tryst.

Lanie stares at me, her eyes scrutinizing, but she doesn't ask any further questions.

Faith senses my unease and changes the subject. "You like Jackson, don't you? He seemed cool to me." She aims her questions at Lanie. I remind myself to thank her later.

"He's amazing, but a perfect gentleman, unfortunately. He didn't even try to kiss me all night, but I guess that's a good sign. Maybe?" Lanie asks, nose scrunched up, begging for validation.

"It's a good sign. He doesn't seem like the typical douche-canoes we meet. Don't act like you don't see he's a total green flag. I mean, you exchanged numbers—you obviously want to see him again." Typical Faith, no sugar-coating.

"It still would have been nice to kiss him at least once, though," Lanie pouts.

I breathe a sigh of relief when the Uber arrives and has third-row seating. I can hide in the back away from any more prying questions.

On the way to Lanie and Faith's apartment, they chatter about the music and club, saying they want to go back on regular nights. Thankfully, I don't need to join in the conversation. My mind is scattered enough at the moment, lost in all things Luke.

Why did he have to be so nice and fun to hang out with? And saying he's sexy doesn't do this man justice. Never mind that mammoth in his pants—I could barely wrap my lips around it. I can still taste him on my tongue.

You're better off alone rather than helping some straight guy figure his shit out, again, only to get fucked over.

We arrive at their apartment in Ballantyne a few minutes after the chatter died down and Lanie rested her head on Faith's shoulder. It's about 2 a.m. and we're all exhausted at this point. Luckily, I live less than ten minutes from them by The Bowl.

Faith shakes Lanie and helps her out of the car. Before they head off, Lanie sticks her head back in. "Goodnight, I love you, and our earlier conversation is not over, brother." She gives me a knowing grin. She's like a Chihuahua with a bone. No way is she going to let this go.

Fuck my life. We're going to get another lecture, aren't we?

Yes, we'll definitely be getting another lecture.

Chapter Ten

MY OBSESSION BEGINS

Luke

Daylight streams through the window of my bedroom as I open my eyes. I check the time to see I only had about three hours' sleep. My internal clock sucks for waking me up so early on a Sunday.

When I got home after 3 a.m. this morning, I couldn't stop thinking about my night with Kaden. I tossed and turned, attempting to fall asleep, without much luck. My last time-check was a little after five this morning, when exhaustion finally took hold of me.

Even now, awake, my thoughts flock to him. Those stunning eyes looked so beautiful with tears flowing from them while he was down on his knees for me. His perfect lips, seemingly at home around my cock, like they were right where they belonged all along. If I didn't already have morning wood, I'd be stiff just from the images flooding my head right now.

I resign myself to getting out of bed, and amble to my ensuite bathroom for my morning routine. Jumping in the shower, I tend to my aching dick that has Kaden's name written all over it. Squeezing some body wash into my hand, I fist my cock and begin lazily stroking while more images of Kaden flash rapidly through my mind. I lean my forearm against the wall, head under the water letting it beat on the nape of my neck and down my back. Remembering the way Kaden let me fuck his face harder than I've ever done to someone has my balls drawing up tight, quicker than normally.

Recalling the sound of his voice saying my name sends tingling sensations down my legs. The way Kaden took charge has me wondering what other filthy orders would leave his mouth if my cock wasn't down his throat. Pumping my fist faster, the only sounds I hear are the water sloshing in sync with it and the guttural groan leaving my throat, cum spewing against the tiled wall. I catch myself when my knees attempt to betray me, falling against the wall.

Geez, what is this guy doing to me?

By the time I finish washing up and get dressed for the day, different images of Kaden have popped up in my memory. The expression on his face when he left the stall, both regretful and worried. The same expression he had when they turned to leave the club for the night. What was he scared of? Me?

He made it clear he was aware I was straight. Obviously, I'm not a run-of-the-mill 'straight guy.' I mean, most straight guys don't follow other guys into the bathroom to get their dicks sucked, right?

Although, I've heard some of Gabe's stories about his 'experimenters' as he referred to them. The so-called straight guys he hooked up with in the clubs he frequented. Is that how Kaden sees me? And why would that scare him?

I guess I am an 'experimenter,' considering last night was my first queer experience. The fact that I liked it speaks volumes. It was more than that, though—I enjoyed Kaden's company equally as much. It was all so easy, and left me wanting a repeat—many, if I'm honest with myself.

I temporarily push all of it to the back of my mind. It's too much for me to unravel right now.

I make my way into the kitchen and hear the tell-tale sound of a neglected cat behind me, meowing because he hasn't been fed as soon as he rolled out of bed. Fred, my ginger Maine Coon, may be the most affectionate cat I've ever met, but when he's hungry, he becomes grumpier than Red Forman on a good day. With the show being a favorite of mine, everyone initially thought I was being creative with the surly character's name, and came up with Fred.

In reality, he was named after this havoc-wreaking character who was an imaginary friend, named Fred, to a little girl in one of my favorite movies as a child. The hippie aunts loved watching old 90s movies when I visited them. My Fred certainly lives up to his namesake's personality if he's not properly fed.

I hastily scoop some of his canned food into his bowl and plop it on the floor for him, filling his water bowl to the brim as well. With a now-happy Fred, peace returns to the room.

The lack of noise leaves me alone with my thoughts, again. They roam back to last night, to him.

Ugh, this is a bigger deal than I first thought.

I attempt to distract myself, collapsing on the couch and opening my laptop to start working on the menu more. We finalized the starters portion a few days ago. Refining those dishes in the kitchen to perfect them starts this week. I've already chosen too many entrées to include on the menu, and I now need to narrow the list down. It's either that or try to reduce the cost of each dish by choosing less expensive items. I would much rather offer fewer choices with higher-quality ingredients, than risk the integrity of my food. You're only as good as your last dish.

I make it through cutting down the entrées and finalizing the salads offered when I startle, my phone's rapid shrills breaking the quiet in my living room. Fred fusses on the couch beside me where he's been resting. Not enjoying the disturbance during his nap, he jumps off the couch and strolls down the hallway toward my bedroom.

I grab my phone and find multiple messages from Jackson. Glancing at the time, I realize I've been working on my menu for a couple hours now.

> is it too soon to call her?

> maybe I should text her first, right?

> what am I thinking of course I should text her

> why would I call her?!

> nobody calls anyone anymore

> we send everyone to vm

> yeah text her. That's totally what I should do

> thanks, bro

I can't help but laugh at the rambling. In classic Jackson fashion, he's having an entire conversation debating with himself in my messages. This may be one of those times where I should save him from his impulsive behavior. Then again, I don't know about dating etiquette anymore. I can't remember the last time I thought about contacting a woman the day after. I wonder if I would want to reach out to Kaden had I gotten his number last night. Fuck, now he's back in my head.

I don't have to wonder too long if I'd contact him—I know. That text would've been sent when I first opened my eyes this morning. I know I shouldn't let anyone divert my focus from the restaurant, but he has me wanting him more than anyone in my past. It's not only the amazing head he gave me—it's surely the best I've ever had—but getting to know him, and seeing him go from shy and awkward, to confident and commanding, was enthralling to say the least.

I meant what I said. When I told him I wasn't done with him, it was equal parts wanting more of him, and hating having been rejected. I'm not used to being dismissed so easily. Especially right after any kind of sexual encounter. Call me childish, but it lit a fire in me, making me *need* for him to want me as much as I want him.

Now my problem is, how do I find a way to see him again? Obviously, I don't have his number or know where he lives. I could see if Jackson could get his number from Lanie for me, but then I'd have to explain why. Somehow, from Kaden's behavior last night I don't think it would be a good idea involving our siblings. I don't know if I'm ready to explain all this to Jackson, either.

What else do I know about him?

Duh, he's a dentist. All I have to do is show up at his office to see him. That's easy enough. One small problem: I don't know his last name. Wait, didn't he say he shares an office with his aunt in Charlotte?

I open the browser and search 'Kaden Dentist Charlotte NC' and cross my fingers. This feels a bit stalkerish, but I'm too nervous about not finding him to care right now. I exhale a sigh of relief when only one result matches. Thank goodness he has a unique first name.

Kaden Parker, D.M.D.

Finding him makes me far more excited than I thought it would. I suddenly have a very bad toothache.

Chapter Eleven

My Lemons Turned Into Lemonade Today

One Month Later

Kaden

S weat is dripping down my temples, the crisp morning air barely keeping me cooled down when I arrive back at my apartment building shortly after six. Every day I seem to be getting out of bed earlier than the previous. The morning makes for the best casual running conditions. Up until a month ago, I was waking up at six to start my routine. I'd perfected my timing so I'd walked into my office a few minutes before nine when my busy day starts.

Then Luke happened. My dreams have been consumed by images of him. His blown-out pupils staring down at me, the moaning he'd tried his best to hold back, hoping he'd please me. Remembering how my throat was sore for days afterwards, but I wasn't complaining. I have no control over when they start, then I wake up in a pool of sweat with my dick harder than the concrete I ran on all morning. It only takes a few minutes to get off after having such vivid dreams, and there's no chance of falling back asleep with lingering thoughts of him.

Now, I'm down to about five hours' sleep if I'm lucky. And instead of my usual thirty minutes, I've had to schedule an hour's lunch in between patients to recuperate at midday. Thankfully, I've been good at keeping my serious doctor pretense on with patients and employees. By the end of my workday, I come home to veg out on the couch, watching old movies while eating takeout until either my sister or friends come to harass me. I think they've come up with a schedule of rotating shifts for each day. Connor and Ender, being in my inner circle of closest friends, as well as Faith and Lanie, have all banded together, trying to pull me out of this funk I've fallen into.

The fucked up thing is, I don't know *why* I'm stuck in this shitty mood. Yes, Luke is on my mind way too often, obviously. But I was the one who drew the line at a one and done. I made the exception with him because, frankly, what sane person could resist him? But why did he have to be so charming, on top of being sexier than any man I've ever met? It's a cruel punishment, for what, I don't know.

To make matters worse, Lanie and Jackson have been inseparable since the party. They started hanging out with each other within days, almost immediately calling themselves exclusive. When she's not here or at work, she's with Jackson. I'm happy for them, truly, but it reminds me more of Luke.

Part of me is jealous of how Jackson texted her the very next day. I didn't give Luke my number, though that was on purpose. You would've thought with his declaration of not being done with me, he would have found a way to contact me by now. I may not have wanted anything more from him after the party, but the fierce determination in his statement and eyes that night did something to me that I can't explain.

My phone ringing in the bedroom pulls me out of my thoughts. I leave my bathroom to finish dressing after my shower, grabbing my water-filled tumbler before answering my phone on speaker.

Right away I know, Lanie has way too much energy for me. "Hey butthead, what do you want for dinner tonight? I'm thinking we should get Bad Daddy's. I'm craving that spicy burger they have, oh and some of their onion rings—they're so fucking good. We have to get some of those. Look at the menu on your lunch break and text me what you want. I'll pick it up on my way to your place."

"Lanie, you don't need to hang out with me tonight. Go over to Jackson's; I'm sure he'll be much better company than me." I pick my phone up off the dresser and make my way out of the house to my car.

"Seriously, Kaden, can I say something to Jackson about Luke now? Please? This is ridiculous. You like him. Stop trying to deny it. You said you had fun with him the night of the party and not only in the men's room." She giggles at herself, her humor about that night breaks up the solemn tone of the conversation. "I know he's supposedly straight, and yes, we hate that. But the way he looked at you that night and what he said to you...I don't know. That doesn't scream 'straight guy' actions to me. Maybe he's worth a shot?" She contemplates this for a moment.

"And I really hate saying that after the lecture I gave you about hooking up with another straight guy. Besides, if he's anything like his brother, he's not a total dickwad like Ty-He Who Shall Not Be Named," Lanie corrects herself.

I sigh heavily. "It doesn't even matter, Lanie. If he wanted to see me like he said he did, he would've asked Jackson for my number. He could have asked you directly. For Goddesses' sake, he could have found me on social media, or by searching for me on the internet. I'm a dentist—it wouldn't be that hard to find me." I sigh in exasperation and regret raising my voice. She doesn't deserve that.

"He's straight. He didn't tell his brother about the night of the party. Which means he plans to remain one-hundred-percent straight. I'll survive this and move on soon enough. I did it last time, and I let that jerk play with my head for almost two years. This is small potatoes compared to him." I don't know if I'm trying to convince her or myself.

Lanie stays quiet, but I can still hear her on the line. As I pull up to my office parking lot, she breaks her silence.

"If it makes you feel any better, Jackson said Luke has been crazy busy preparing for the opening of his restaurant. He hasn't even seen Luke more than once in the past month. Maybe he's just busy?" She's grasping at straws, trying to make me feel better. It doesn't help, but I love her more for trying.

I refuse to delude myself, though. "Lanie, I'm at the office. I have to get inside, but I'll see you tonight. Love you." I wait long enough to hear her say, "I love you," then end the call.

Walking into the office, Kelsey, my personal assistant, greets me with her usual bright smile. She's so sweet that it sometimes makes *my* teeth hurt to interact with her.

Don't take it out on her because you decided to torment yourself over another straight guy.

Aunt Olivia and I have our own personal assistants, on top of our mutual staff. Kelsey has been good to me since I've joined the practice. I don't have to worry about much with her here to keep things in order. Kelsey has been managing the office alone while my aunt and her assistant both took vacations this week, and I remind myself to get her a nice gift for her birthday in a couple months.

Turning on my happy switch, I step up to the counter with a forced smile to review my appointment book for the day.

"Good morning, Dr. Parker! Did you get some good rest last night?" Kelsey disguises her question as small talk instead of concern for the shadows that have begun to form under my eyes.

"Feeling good, thanks for asking. Solid seven hours—can't complain." I lie to ease her worrying.

She's not fooled, but carries on with a slight nod as she shows me what's on the books for today. Looks like I've got a full day ahead of me, which means I'll get to stay busy and keep my mind from wandering. Sounds good to me.

Noticing the four o'clock time slot this afternoon causes me to catch my breath.

New Patient: Alden Stonewood

It takes me a few seconds to register the first name on the list. I shake off the intrusive thoughts of Luke, trying to push their way into my head, then finish prepping for the day with Kelsey before making my way back to my office.

Lanie mentioned Jackson's last name during a conversation with our parents last week at Sunday dinner. I absolutely *did not* remember it for any other reason than to know who my sister spends her time with, for safety reasons.

Sure, Kaden.

Fine, I may have stalked him on social media. I'm not proud of myself, but at least I learned he doesn't really date. There were no photos of him with women, besides a few with two older women who looked more like a couple themselves. It seems his entire online presence revolves around food or building his restaurant. I can't say I was upset by my findings.

I make it through the day without falling on my face from exhaustion. I managed to get a quick nap in on my lunch break, my head nestled in my arms on my desk. Not the most comfortable way to rest, but when you're desperate, you can't be picky.

I'm about to leave my office to go into my final appointment for the day, when two hygienists coming down the hallway, whispering and giggling, draw my attention.

"Did you see his eyes?" Amanda whispers to Courtney. "Gorgeous!"

"His eyes? I was too distracted by those biceps covered in tattoos, and don't even get me started on that ass." Courtney makes an 'oof' sound, fanning herself as they walk past my door.

"Good afternoon, ladies." They startle, hastily turning around to face me, realizing I heard their conversation about a patient.

"Uh, hi, Dr. Parker. Your last appointment is waiting in Room Three for you," Amanda rattles off nervously.

"Thank you, Amanda," I reply with a stern look from one to the other, reminding them to use discretion while patients are still in the building. They know better than this. With a nod they both scurry off to their stations. I hate being a hard-ass at work, but things like that could get us all in trouble had the patient overheard them instead of me.

I grab the clipboard from the bin outside Room Three as I walk in to meet my new patient.

I only get two steps into the room before I freeze in place, staring into those same jade-green soul-stealers that have haunted my dreams for the past month.

"Hey, Just the Brother. Fancy meeting you here."

What the fuck?

Chapter Twelve

My Day Can't Get Any Better Than This

Luke

The stunned look on Kaden's face was worth the wait. When I called for an appointment with his office, the scheduler said they were booked solid for over a month for new patients. My appointment was set for mid-February, so I was ecstatic when I got a call on Monday asking if I'd like this time slot, two weeks earlier than my original one, because they'd had a cancellation. I wanted to see him so badly, but I didn't want to ask Jackson or Lanie for his number. I definitely wasn't going to approach him randomly outside his office, because that's not weird *at all*.

I'm not proud of how much I've stalked him online, trying to learn everything I can about him. I couldn't help myself. Late nights working on planning and building the restaurant has me coming home wired, sleep nowhere in sight until I unwind from the hectic day. Lying in bed, getting to know Kaden from afar, was better than doom-scrolling any d ay.

The photos on his social media don't do him justice. In his current state of shock, he's still gorgeous. The scrubs he's wearing make him seem younger than when we first met. His face, now void of any color, tells me he's freaked out by me showing up here. I attempt, and fail at, avoiding checking him out. It's too hard to stop ogling his physique, appreciating the view. He looks *really* good in those scrubs. I can't help but notice how tired he looks, though.

He slow-blinks a few times, the shock finally wearing off, "Luke, what are you doing here? Did you lie about your name on my records, so I didn't know it was you?" Kaden closes the door behind him, taking a few more steps into the room, finishing his last question when the door shuts completely.

"Not at all. Alden is my legal name, after my grandfather. Luke is my middle name, which suits me much better, don't you think?" I flash my flirtiest grin his way.

He seems lost for words, an empty stare aimed at me.

"Don't you need to ask me some questions? Past dental history? What brings me here today? Are there any family medical issues we should be concerned about? Aren't those standard doctor questions?" I attempt to help him past the awkwardness of the moment.

"Luke, don't play with me. We both know you didn't come here for dental work." Now out of his stupor, he sounds almost annoyed with me.

"Hey now, that's not true. I have some major tooth pain going on. My old dentist retired, so I went looking for a new one. How was I supposed to know this was your office?" I get a skeptic, one-sided smirk.

A crack in the ice. That's something!

"C'mon doc, I'm suffering. Give a guy a break."

"Luke why are you here?" His voice sounds sullen now.

I attempt some sincerity instead. "I wanted to see you, Kaden. I didn't have your number. I wasn't sure if your sister knew what happened between us or if you wanted her to know, so I didn't ask her. I felt hanging out in the parking lot of your office was way more stalkerish than I'm comfortable with. C'mon, doc, I'm at your mercy, begging you to help me with my pain."

Kaden's gaze is laced with suspicion as he takes a few steps closer to where I'm sitting. "And what kind of pain are you in exactly?"

"I'm not entirely sure, but about a month ago, some...*thing* caught hold of me, and now I can't get it out from under my skin—I mean gums. It's a really weird feeling. I've never felt anything like it. Can you help me with it, doc? The pain, that is."

There it is. I missed that dimple. My stomach does that thing you feel during the big drop on a roller coaster.

His amusement shines through his smile. "Pain is your friend; it's your humanity. Pain makes you interesting."

"I think I just fell in love with you," I whisper aloud, not comprehending the gravity of the words leaving my mouth. Kaden's stunned expression makes me hastily retract my statement.

"Uh, I didn't mean to...That wasn't what I..." I stumble over my words, dropping my chin to my chest in embarrassment. Fuck, it's not like anything I say could make what I said seem any less crazy.

Owning up to it, I make eye contact again, and question in disbelief, "You quoted Janie from Drop Dead Fred. I *love* that movie. My aunts made me watch it so many times growing up. I still can't get through the movie without laughing until my cheeks hurt." I smile, remembering the afternoons sitting on the couch, eating popcorn, and laughing like we couldn't stop ourselves even if we tried. It eases some of the nervousness running through me.

"First you quote SpongeBob, now one of my favorite movies. It's like you've hacked my brain." My playfulness helps melt away the shocked look on his face.

Kaden smirks, stepping closer and leaning forward to whisper in my ear, "I guess a good blowjob can do the trick." Pulling away, leaving his scent lingering behind, he hits me like a freight train with those seductive eyes, drawing out all the air from my lungs.

Well, hello there, my brazen Kaden. Nice of you to join us.

58

All nervousness is officially gone. I glance up at him through my lashes, and rephrase for him. "You mean an *amazing* blowjob. Don't downplay your expertise at sucking my cock, Kaden." I'm surprised at the gravel in my voice.

"Oh, I wasn't downplaying—only letting you confirm we're on the same page." His sultry gaze has blood rushing to my dick. "I know exactly how well I sucked your cock, Luke. That's really why you're here, isn't it? Tell me, did your brother have to remind you what your name was on the way home?" He's standing in front of me, knee-to-knee, peering down with a devilish grin.

"It actually took me three days to remember my name, but who's counting? And while I tremendously enjoyed your exceptional skills in sucking pertinent information out of me through my cock and would *never* decline an offer for a repeat, that's not the reason I'm here." I unsubtly press my palm against my bulging cock, pleased with myself that it doesn't go unnoticed.

The stimulating exchange sends my brain into overdrive with images of him on his knees, making me crave the feeling of my dick down his throat right here and now.

"Then you'll have to tell me why you're really here, so I can determine if said repeat can be offered." Kaden doesn't let up on the seductive banter.

As much as I'm enjoying this, my dick is already too hard. This is not the time or place to alleviate the discomfort it's causing me. I decide to give in and be direct. "I'd like you to have dinner with me. Tonight. If you don't have any plans, that is."

The vacant stare is back. "I don't think that's such a good idea, Luke."

"Would you care to elaborate *why* you think it's not a good idea?"

He backs away from me, looking around nervously instead of answering my question. This hot and cold is starting to confuse the fuck out of me. One minute he's flirting heavily with me, but when I genuinely tell him I want to see him again, he clams up. Why is he opposed to whatever this is between us?

I cautiously break the silence, attempting to ease his hesitation. "Kaden, it's only dinner. It doesn't have to be anything more if that's what you need from me. I think we both enjoyed each other's company the night we met, right? I know I did."

He thinks it over for a second, giving me a slow nod in agreement.

"Good, then this doesn't need to be a big deal. Dinner between new friends. If that's all you have to give me, then I'll gladly accept it." I attempt to meet him halfway. It's obvious he has major reservations about anything more, no matter how playful he was a few minutes ago.

He's quiet for a minute, clearly debating with himself before responding to my proposition. "Okay, Luke. Dinner. *Just* dinner." Kaden's cautious words are followed by that beautiful smile, while his penetrating eyes seem to connect with my very soul.

The roller coaster has dropped beneath me, leaving me soaring wildly with no regard for the misery I'm about to endure by the constraints I've put on us.□

Any part of Kaden is better than none at all.

Chapter Thirteen

I Might Lose My Sanity Today

Kaden

Dinner. That's all I've committed to, nothing more.

Keep telling yourself that.

Why can't I have dinner with him? There's no reason why we can't be friends. Just because you sucked some guy's dick doesn't mean you can't be friends with him. I've fucked around with Ender in the past and he's still in the inner circle. It's fine. Everything's fine.

I finish my end of day tasks in a hurry. Leaving my office a few minutes past 4:30 p.m., I walk out to the lobby to make sure Kelsey doesn't need anything else from me. I find her watching me with a grin.

"I'm going to head out a little early—you good to handle closing up when everyone leaves?" I ask her.

Her eyes bounce from me to the waiting room then back to me, her grin widening. I glance toward the waiting room and find Luke looking like a giant sitting in a chair, staring at his phone.

"Yes, Dr. Parker. I'm all set. Have a nice night!" She's way too excited for me to leave with Luke. Ms. Nosy Body thinks this is more than what it really is—dinner, with a friend. That's it. I remind myself to cancel that birthday present.

Stop it, Kaden.

Luke's head pops up when he hears Kelsey say my name. He flashes that perfect smile at me, and his bright eyes lock on mine, causing the tiniest whimper to leave my mouth.

My hand flies to my lips while I swing my head toward Kelsey to see if she noticed. My ears burn like fire when I see her beaming with enthusiasm. It's as if she's in on the bet with Lanie and Faith.

I shake my head. "Goodnight, Kelsey."

"Goodnight, Dr. Parker," Kelsey replies, more formally this time.

Luke stands and joins me, walking toward the door. I can't help appreciating how well his black short-sleeve Henley forms around his muscular chest and biceps. The faded jeans he's wearing are just as snug, looking like they were painted on. Though I can't see his ass as he walks beside me, I remember the ample hardened curves under my hands that night in the stall. I see why Courtney was overheated. My gut twists just imagining what she may have been thinking about him.

Jealous much?

"Do you mind if I drive?" he asks, opening the door for me. The soft whoosh of warm air that comes through it is evidence of the inconsistent weather in North Carolina during the winter months. Leave the house with a jacket on, come home with it over your shoulder.

I nod, saying, "That's fine. Can we stop by my place so I can change out of my scrubs?"

"You look good in scrubs, but whatever you're more comfortable in."

I struggle not to react to the fluttering in my stomach.

Before the door can fully close behind us, I hear a cheerful voice from inside. "Have a nice evening, Mr. Stonewood."

I swear, I'm firing her tomorrow.

No, you're not.

Luke chuckles and gives a slight wave through the glass window. "She's a little invested in how you spend your personal time, huh?"

"She's harmless. As much as I'd like to fire her at the moment, I know she cares enough to want me to be happy."

"Are you not happy?" His quizzical eyes meet mine as we get to his Jeep Wrangler, opening the passenger door for me.

I look at his hand holding the door, then back to his face. "Do you always open car doors for your male friends, Luke?"

"Do you always avoid answering questions that make you uncomfortable, Kaden?" He challenges me with a smirk.

"Now look who's avoiding questions." My retort gets a laugh from Luke. He doesn't let go of the door. I give in and gracefully take my seat, letting him close the door for me.

The door is halfway closed when Luke leans his head in near my ear, "Only male friends who've had their mouth around my cock." I can still feel his warm breath against my skin as he closes the door, my mouth agape.

Dear Goddesses, please help me get through this night without ripping this man's clothes off.

After Luke plugs my address into his Jeep's GPS, we're silent on the drive to my apartment. Not necessarily uncomfortably, but my brain is still reeling on the events this afternoon thus far.

Luke showing up was the last thing on my radar for the day. I can't say I'm disappointed in the least. I've been miserable the past month. Much to my disappointment, he hadn't attempted to contact me. Now that he's here I actually have to decide what I want out of this...thing between us. Can I be friends with him and not get distracted by how fucking much I want him? The immeasurable compulsions I'm having to strip this man bare, bend him over, repeatedly ram my cock into his ass until he can't sit for days, have me thinking it's not possible.

My breath hitches at the visuals flashing through my mind. Heat swarms the nape of my neck.

"That's a lot of thinking going on over there. Anything fun?" Luke smirks as if knowing where my mind has been.

"Uh, nothing. I remembered I forgot to lock my office door."

"You sure? You look a little red in the face. Do you need some air? You can roll down your window if you're hot," he offers, feigning concern.

"I'm fine, Luke. I'm not hot, don't worry."

"I beg to differ," Luke mumbles as we pull up to my building. I ignore his quip for my own good.

"It'll only take me a few minutes to change." The engine shuts down. I turn to see him unbuckling his seatbelt, grabbing the door handle to push it open.

"Where are you going?"

"In-side-to-wait-for-you-to-fin-ish-chang-ing," Luke slowly enunciates each syllable, brows scrunched as if I asked a foolish question.

"No!" I blurt out instinctively. There's no way I can have this man alone in my apartment with me right now, especially while I have to take my clothes off to change. Talk about self-sabotage!

"Stay. Don't move," I tell him, pointing my finger at his seat as to reinforce my instructions.

The cheeky bastard looks me dead in the eyes and woofs like a dog, "Yes, sir."

I feel my nostrils flare as my cock twitches to life from the imagery.

"Or do you prefer, 'Yes, daddy'?"

He's trying to fucking kill us and we haven't even eaten dinner yet.

"No." I turn away and leave the Jeep without another word, hearing him chuckle as I swing the door shut in frustration. If he knows what's good for him, he'll stay right the fuck there.

I wonder if I have enough time to jerk off in the shower and get dressed before he thinks I've ditched him and leaves.

If you don't do it, he'll be in your bed pounding you into the mattress by the end of the night.

The jury is still out on which option is the 'least likely to break Kaden's heart.'

Chapter Fourteen

He Makes Me Want More

Luke

A lmost thirty minutes have passed when Kaden finally comes back out of his building. I would have gone in there to look for him, but I knew there was no way I'd find him even if I could get in the lobby doors.

He looks comfortable in jeans and a polo shirt, and I'm glad to see he brought a light jacket that he's holding over his arm. A good sign he plans on letting me keep him out late enough to get cold and have to wear it.

Climbing into the Jeep, he side-eyes me, "Hey, sorry I took so long. Had to make a call to Lanie and let her know my plans changed for tonight. Hope you weren't too bored."

His hair is wet, and his skin is flushed. he's facing forward out the windshield, purposely not looking my way.

"Did you shower?"

He glances at me. "Yeah. I felt grimy from being around people all day. I had to quickly rinse off." He fake-smiles at the windshield.

I contemplate not asking, but ultimately can't resist. "Did you take a shower so you could jerk off, Kaden?" I do my best to hide how amused I am.

Still facing forward, he makes a request that sounds more like a command. "Can we get going? I'm getting really hungry and I haven't eaten since breakfast."

I barely stifle the laughter trying to escape my throat. "Sure, I'm hungry too." I decide to let this one go for now.

He remains quiet on our way to the restaurant, so I put some music on to ease the discomfort. I hope I didn't hurt his feelings or embarrass him. I don't want to make a big deal about it, but I also don't want to be a total dick.

"If it makes you feel any better, I rubbed one out before I went to your office," I tell him with a smirk, and nudge him with my elbow over the armrest.

"Well, at least I wasn't the reason you had to do it. It was your relentless teasing that made it necessary, otherwise we may not have made it to the restaurant." The indignation in his voice makes me chuckle.

"First of all, who said you weren't the reason I had to come before seeing you today? And I would love to hear more about why we wouldn't have made it to the restaurant. That sounds *very* interesting."

Kaden rolls his eyes and gives a muffled laugh, shaking his head at me. "You're persistent; I'll give you that."

"Like I said," I tell him with certainty, "when I know what I want, I go after it."

Kaden's eyes meet mine for the first time since he got back into the Jeep. I don't know what to make of the bewildered expression on his face, so I direct my attention back to the road instead.

Fortunately, we arrive at the restaurant a minute later. I park and jump out to open Kaden's door, only to wind up meeting him in front. I'm suddenly nervous, like I need to be careful how far I push him.

We walk to the restaurant side-by-side, and I have to shove my hands into my pockets to keep them from where they instinctively want to go.

I grab the door, opening it to let him walk through first. He allows it, giving me a slight smile and nodding in appreciation.

"Welcome to Red Oak Steakhouse! Do you have a reservation?" The host's sunny personality snaps me out of my head.

"Yes, Stonewood—party of two."

"Ah, yes. I have your table ready for you. Follow me please."

I make a path for Kaden to follow the host first, resting my hand on his lower back. I feel him inhale sharply at the touch, and I quickly drop my hand.

"When did you make a reservation? Did you assume I wouldn't say no?" Kaden whispers accusingly.

"More like hoping and preparing in case I got lucky." I see the corner of his lip raise the slightest bit. I'll take it.

"Here we are." The host places our menus on the table. "Your server this evening will be Mia. I'll let her know you've arrived."

We take our seats and start looking through the menu when I catch him glancing at me over the top of his.

"Good evening, gentlemen. My name is Mia, and I'll be your server tonight." Mia introduces herself as she pours water in our glasses. "Can I get you something to drink to start? We have a large wine selection in the back of the menu."

I decide to order first, since I'm getting the feeling Kaden is uncomfortable with me treating him like my date.

"Hi Mia. I'd love a glass of Cabernet Sauvignon, please." I give a friendly smile and turn toward him.

"I'll have the same, thank you, Mia." Kaden says to her, his eyes returning all too quickly to mine.

I don't hear Mia leave as we enter a standoff, neither of us wanting to back down from the intense eye contact we've fallen into.

After a minute that felt like an hour, Kaden breaks the silence. "What are you doing, Luke?" His tone is skeptical.

Confused by the question, I take my usual route, leading with humor. "I'm about to order a steak so rare it's one chest pump away from slapping a bell on it and putting it back out in the pasture."

Kaden laughs loudly, drawing attention from other diners, causing him to slap a hand across his mouth to stifle the disturbance. Before he can stop himself, I find myself joining, his smile and laugh being too infectious to resist.

"You're something else, Mr. Stonewood, you know that?"

"Eww, don't call me that. Sounds too serious to be coming from you. Hard pass." Aiming to continue breaking down that wall he built up earlier, I stay with the humorous approach. "I'd rather you stick to something more flattering, like Big Guy or Stud Muffin. Oh wait, how about Snugglebug? I'm an expert at snuggling. Yep, I like that one. Let's go with that."

Kaden's shoulders visibly shake as he fights to contain his laughter. His smile is slowly becoming my new favorite thing in the world, and I love being the one to draw it out of him.

Soon, Mia shows up with our wine and takes our orders. I'm impressed when Kaden orders his steak medium-rare. If he'd asked for it well-done, I'd have no choice but to walk out of the restaurant, my head hanging in shame.

Now we're alone once again, steadily watching each other grinning from ear-to-ear.

"Tell me something I don't know about you," I ask him.

"What do you want to know, Luke?"

"Everything." I'm not going to get what I want all at once, so I make the effort to be practical. "But let's start with your favorite childhood memory."

"That's easy. Sunday dinner and game nights," Kaden says with no hesitation.

"Tell me more."

"When my mom was a kid, my grandparents worked a lot. They weren't the 'sit down at the table and eat dinner every night' type of family. When my mom had my sister and I, she decided she didn't want that for us. I was about five years old when it became mandatory to have a sit-down dinner with all four of us. Of course, there were times when one of my parents had to work late or whatnot, but they did their best to make sure it was an almost every night occurrence."

"And I suppose that morphed into Sunday dinner and game night at some point?" I question, more than curious.

"Yeah, once we got older and started having social lives and wanted to hang out with our friends all the time. Typical teenage stuff. My parents agreed to a deviation—on one condition, we make it Sunday dinner and game night every weekend. Lanie and I agreed, reluctantly because of the board games part of the deal. After the first few games my dad introduced us to on those nights, it became our favorite part of the week. Spending time laughing, and of course, shit talking about who's going to win the games, turned out to be a lot of fun."

"Sounds like you all are close. When did your parents let you out of the deal?"

"I'll let you know when they do," Kaden chuckles at his jest.

"Really? You both still go to your parents' house every Sunday for dinner, and play board games?"

"Every Sunday. We love it, honestly. My parents are really fun to hang out with. Is that weird to say?" He smiles shyly, lowering his head like it's embarrassing to admit.

"Not at all. You're pretty lucky. Some people wish they had that kind of relationship with their family. You should be proud."

Raising his head again, his eyes meet mine as I nod in assurance.

I'm one of those people.

I want to tell him but now is not the time to dump all my family baggage on him. I don't want to scare him off before we even get a chance to get to know each other better.

"Your turn. Favorite childhood memory?" Kaden asks before I can get another question for him out—I have many.

"A few weeks after I turned ten years old, my Aunt Brenda was in the kitchen cooking dinner for a couple of her friends coming over that night. She was making fried chicken and mashed potatoes. I always liked watching her cook. It seemed...peaceful. She'd never let me help until then, worried I would make too much of a mess. She asked me to help season the breading mixture for the chicken—because seasoning the buttermilk was not enough—she always said, then she handed me the masher for the potatoes." I smile, remembering how she faked her hands hurting so she had an excuse to ask me to mash the potatoes. "At the dinner table, she gave all the credit to me when everyone said the food was delicious. I think that's the moment I fell in love with cooking. People enjoying something you created. I guess you could say my aunt letting me feel useful turned out to be the start of my career. I dove headfirst into watching every cooking show I could find, helping both my aunts with dinner on the nights I spent with them. Cooking consumed my every waking thought, and still does." I pause, then reconsider. "Well, every waking thought until recently, that is." I gesture toward him with an open hand.

"Unapologetically straightforward as ever, huh?" Kaden shakes his head with a smile.

"I'm not one for subtlety. I don't have time in my life for nonsense," I say with sincerity. I'm still not sure how a little over a month ago, I was ready to die on the 'I don't want to be in a relationship' hill, but now here I am, willingly running down said hill, directly toward Kaden.

Chapter Fifteen

I Wasn't Really Hungry
Anyway

Kaden

When I think I have a grasp on who Luke is, he presents a different side of himself. All afternoon he's been playful and flirty, now he's casting the same determination he had in his eyes the night we met, my way. That night I figured it was rejection in his stare. It isn't this time. I stare back, unable to form words.

Mia conveniently arrives with our food, giving me a chance to focus on something else besides the thunderous hammering in my ribcage.

I take a deep breath and thank Mia along with the obligatory, "This looks delicious," statement.

We both begin eating our meals, hopefully leaving that conversation behind. We're surrounded by noise, yet we sit in a comfortable silence.

"Is your steak still mooing? Do you need me to hit it over the head for you?" I ask playfully.

"It's perfect. The mooing is barely audible," Luke smirks, shoving a piece of steak into his mouth. I chuckle and reach for my wine glass.

My eyes peek over the rim of the glass, wandering from his eyes down to those sinful lips as he slowly pulls the fork out.

I've never wanted to be an inanimate object so much in all my life.
Did he just moan?

Blood rushes to my dick. Flames ignite where my ears used to be. I've all but stopped breathing.

"Sorry, the steak is really good. It's hard for me to stay quiet when I'm really enjoying something." This man has the audacity to wink, after reminding me of how hard it was for him to stay silent while he mouthfucked me. He's not fighting fair at all. The man knows what he's doing to me and doesn't regret a single second of it.

Two can play this game.

I place my glass down and spear my own piece of steak. "That's a good quality to have. I like to hear a man growling and grunting like an animal as he pummels my ass with his enormous cock, pulling my hair and rearranging my insides until I can't walk the next day," I say nonchalantly, not caring who else heard me. I place the steak in my mouth and remove the fork as slow as possible. For added effect, I roll my eyes and let out the slightest whimper.

When I finish my act of retribution, I open my eyes and continue eating my meal like nothing happened.

A full minute goes by with nothing but crickets on his end, and when I look up, it's to an entirely different Luke. Lips clenched shut and nostrils flaring like a bull chasing his target, his eyes are filled with primal lust as he fists his dinner napkin in one hand, the other tightly clenched around his fork. The rise and fall of his shoulders has intensified enough that it's attracted curious looks from nearby diners.

I. Am. Speechless.

With the worst timing ever, Mia comes to check on us. Poor girl takes one look at Luke, and then at me, seeing us in our current standoff and turns back around, walking away without saying a word.

Luke breaks first, placing his fork and napkin carefully on the table. "Kaden, I'm going to step away to the restroom for a couple minutes. When I get back, I'd really like it if you could have the check paid so I can take you back to my place and spend the night achieving my new goal of making you incapable of walking tomorrow." He's barely composed enough to tell me his intentions while slowly taking out his wallet and handing me his credit card. Without another word, he stands and makes his way toward the back of the restaurant.

We may have played that game a little too well.

Don't overthink this. It doesn't have to mean anything. If it doesn't mean anything, I won't want to do it again. I can get him out of my system and be done with him. Straight guy problem solved.

"Sound logic," said no sane person ever.

We're in too deep for that justification.

I wave down Mia, handing her the card without even waiting for the check.

As I finish forging Luke's signature on the bill, I feel him arrive back at the table, hovering next to me. Standing slowly, I grab my jacket and hand him his card.

His wild eyes laser-focused on mine, Luke takes the card from my hand and puts it in his back pocket. His other hand grabs mine, entwining our fingers before all but dragging me out of the restaurant.

We may be close in height, but I still have trouble keeping up with his pace. Arriving at the passenger side of his Jeep, I assume he's opening the door for me. Instead, he spins me, pinning my back to the door, chest to chest. His lips crash into mine, fingers snaking behind my neck, his thumb pinned to my jaw. His other hand finds its way onto the bare skin at the bottom of my back, causing goosebumps to form over my entire body. The kiss is sudden and rough. Lips pressed hard against mine, desperate for the connection.

We remain fused as one until he's had his fill. Like a starved man finding contentment after being given what he was deprived of for so long, he breathes in deeply, releasing it with a sigh. His lips turn gentle against mine, tongue swiping across my lips. They intuitively part, inviting him in.

The butterflies return with vigor. I sigh, welcoming them.

My hands find their place on his hips, pulling him to me so that our confined cocks are pressed firmly against each other. Luke grunts at the abrupt connection, changing our caressing tongues into a battle for control, his fingers now gripping the skin above the waistline of my jeans hard enough that I know there'll be bruises tomorrow. I can't wait to see his marks on me.

Laughter from other patrons of the restaurant in the parking lot bring our attention back to our surroundings. Luke pulls back from my lips, leaving his forehead resting against mine, our heaving breaths mingling in the space between us.

"Tell me no, and I'll put a stop to this right now. If I hear any other words from your mouth other than no, I am putting you in this truck and taking you to my bed." Luke gives me an out, revealing he's noticed my repeated hesitation to pursue this any further.

I surrender to him. "*Just* this once."

Chapter Sixteen

My Day In Fact Got Better

Luke

Just this once.

I can think about his answer later. All I know right now is it wasn't 'no.'

Pulling him away from the door to open it for him, I gently nudge him into his seat, reaching over and engaging his seatbelt.

Then I climb into the driver's seat as fast as I can. My apartment is only about ten minutes away, thankfully, because I'm not sure I can keep my hands off him for much longer.

My brain has been completely malfunctioning since the mindfuck Kaden delivered went straight to my cock. His playful admission was so unexpected that it threw me for a loop. At first, I was frozen, speechless. Then came the image of Kaden laid out bare on my bed, looking at me with that seductive expression that crosses his face sometimes without him even noticing he's doing it. Before I could shake myself of my stupor, my head was flooded with a vision of Kaden in front of me, ass in the air, letting me make every filthy detail of his lewd confession come true.

Then Mia came to the table, bringing me back to reality, and I had to get away from him for a minute to collect myself. I gave him the only scenario that was consuming my thoughts at that moment.

Walking to the restroom, my internal battle began. I went to Kaden's office today with the full intention of taking him to dinner and getting to know him better. When I'd told Gabe I'd met someone who caught my interest, he'd been skeptical-only because until now, I'd been adamant about my no-relationship rule while I focus on the restaurant opening and turning it into a success. You can imagine how mind-blowing it had been for him when I'd revealed that person is a man. While telling Gabe all about Kaden, sans our tryst in the restroom, I'd been giddy, remembering how much I'd enjoyed his company. It was the first time I'd wanted to spend more time with someone—a lot more. I hadn't realized I was lonely until I'd met someone who made me feel *something*, and not merely lust—more than that.

Hearing Kaden tell me what he likes from a partner in bed made my cock instantly rock hard. I'd debated back and forth with myself in the restroom, deciding whether to go through with the new plan for the night my cock had come up with. I don't want Kaden thinking I came to see him to get off and leave.

When I got back to the table, he had followed through with my request, ready to leave with me. That solidified the decision-he wants this as much as I do. I'll have to show him that I want much more than this tomorrow. I *need* him to know I want more of him in my life, in so many ways. Tonight, I'll show him I can fulfill his desires, leaving him satisfied in bed before I pursue him in every other way.

The whole ride to my place, Kaden is quiet, leaving me to stew alone in the chaos running through my mind. When I finally pull into my building's parking lot, I refocus my thoughts onto what we're both intending to happen when we get inside, and hurriedly help Kaden out of the passenger side. I graze my lips across that sweet spot below his ear, then intertwine our fingers once again with the intent of escorting him directly to my bedroom.

I don't think I've ever wanted someone as much as I want him. *Need him.* My mind has one track right now, and it's focused solely on getting inside Kaden.

We make our way into the building. In the elevator my mouth frantically finds his as soon as the doors close, trapping his body between mine. Our cocks rest against each other, his now as hard as mine has been since I left for the restroom in the restaurant.

The doors open again all too quickly, and I lead the way down the hall to my door. Never letting go of his hand, I unlock the door with the keys in my free hand, towing him in and kicking the door shut behind us. I take the direct route to my bedroom, not bothering to acknowledge that the rest of the apartment exists.

Slamming my bedroom door shut, I push Kaden against the door while I accost every inch of his exposed skin with my mouth, sucking and biting his lips and neck while my hands desperately undress him. I throw his shirt somewhere to the side and begin to undo his jeans when I feel his hand come between us.

His palm softly pushes against my chest, barely separating our bodies. Our lips break contact as I stare at him wondering if he's changed his mind.

Instead of telling me with words what he wants, his fingers grasp the hem of my Henley and pull it over my head, winding up somewhere on the floor. He unshackles my rock-hard cock from its confinement inside my jeans and boxer briefs, which join the rest of our clothes on the floor.

His tongue begins its journey, starting at my neck below my ear, as he makes his way down past my collarbone, pausing to give special attention to each nipple before continuing further, nibbling and biting along the way. My hands roam through his messy hair, loving the feel of it, as his hands caress every part of my body his mouth doesn't reach. My chest swells from more than physical sensations.

Once again, I'm gifted with the sight of Kaden on his knees, gazing up at me with hooded eyes. It takes my breath away. I plant one palm on the door in front of me, while the other tangles itself tighter in his hair.

"I wish you could see how beautiful you look down there."

The tip of his tongue circles the head of my cock, paying special attention to the ridge on the underside, and sending shivers down my spine. I encourage him, moving my hand from his hair to his chin, pulling it down and pushing my hips forward. He doesn't waste any time, repeatedly taking me to the back of his throat and hollowing his cheeks as he pulls away again to wrap his lips around the head. I can feel myself getting closer to the edge. I pull all the way out of his mouth and haul him up onto his feet before I come too soon—I don't want this to end yet.

Attempting to regain my composure, I force out two, barely recognizable words. "Bed. Now." I briefly press my lips to his, then back away to the bed, taking him with me hand-in-hand.

As soon as we hit the bed, he pushes me down onto my back, nodding for me to move further toward the headboard. Crawling onto the bed and straddling me, he spits into his hand before capturing my mouth with his once again. His spit-soaked hand comes between us, wrapping around both our cocks as he begins thrusting into it.

Overwhelmed with the sensations coursing through my body, I pull back from the tongue-fucking he's giving my mouth and look down at his hand around us. My eyes stay fixed there, entranced by the sight of his cock thrusting against mine, his wrist twisting and thumb grazing over both our heads with each stroke.

With my breaking point nearing, my movements are too quick, making Kaden let out an 'oomph' as I wrap an arm tightly around his waist and flip him onto his back, leaving me positioned on top of him between his legs.

I drop my body onto him, trapping his hand so it can't continue its assault on my sanity.

"If I don't get inside you right now, we're going to have a problem," I say breathlessly as I reach to the nightstand for lube and a condom.

"I have to prep myself first," Kaden says softly, taking the lube from my hand.

I roll back onto my haunches between his legs. He looks at me tentatively before squeezing the lube onto his fingers and raising his knees to his chest. I help him, my hands smoothing along the backs of his thighs, holding them in place.

My attention hones in on Kaden's index finger circling his hole, pushing in, and slowly pumping inside himself. My hands instinctively tighten around his thighs, but I force myself to relax, not wanting to hurt him. I start massaging his thighs and the curves of his ass, mesmerized by his middle finger now joining his index. Then a third, thrusting faster, stretching him.

Kaden lets out a whimper, pulling my gaze up to his face. His eyes are scrunched, and mouth gaping open, and I almost come on the spot.

His eyes fly open, and his fingers slide out of him. "Need you, now."

Grabbing the condom from the side of the bed, I unwrap it and roll it down my shaft. I slick myself up with lube and nudge Kaden's leg.

"On your stomach," I order. He promptly complies pushing his ass up in the air, elbows and forehead against the mattress.

I position my cock, slowly pushing the head in until it breaches his outer ring of muscle. I pump in and out a few times, sinking further in each time. My eyes are fixed on our connection. Hypnotized by the way his asshole is sucking my cock in like its opening a door for me to come home. Kaden makes a sound resembling both pain and pleasure at the same time, snapping my attention away.

"Are you okay? I'm not sure if that was a good or bad sound. I don't want to hurt you. Did I hurt you?" I rapid-fire the panicked thoughts in my head, remaining completely still.

"That was a good sound. Keep going, don't stop." He takes deep breaths with me seated halfway inside him.

I rub a hand up and down his spine, the other holding onto his hip. I continue slowly pushing into him until my balls are resting against his. His ass is gripping my cock so tight in its warmth that it sends an electrical current humming beneath my skin, surging through every nerve in my body.

My turn to take some deep breaths. "Warning you now, I don't know how long I'm going to last. You feel so good I can't even describe it. Give me a second, don't move."

I fold over him, resting both hands on his hips, my forehead on his shoulder blade. Kaden gives a soft chuckle, followed by his ass clenching in succession hard around my cock. The act of defiance makes my body jerk up from the added pressure. Without thinking, my hand lands palm flat against his asscheek with a loud 'whack.'

Kaden jerks forward with a gasp followed by a soft sigh, pulling me halfway out of him with the movement. I grab both his hips and slam forward, making Kaden groan loudly as he drops his head into the mattress.

I snicker at his reaction. "Seems to me someone likes being punished for being a brat."

"It's cute you think that's a punishment," he retorts, looking over his shoulder with a devilish grin.

"Let's see if you're still smiling when you can't walk tomorrow." Without warning, I start pounding into him relentlessly with one goal in mind—make him remember.

The room is filled with the carnal sound of skin slapping against skin. Kaden seems to only know the words 'fuck yes' now, along with low moans, while I'm having trouble controlling the grunts and heavy panting from the effort. Two things off the checklist he created for me in the restaurant. Sweat begins to form all over my body, and my grip tightens around his hips to maintain rhythm. I can already see the red marks they're leaving which will turn into bruises tomorrow. The thought of him having a physical reminder of the savage fucking he's currently receiving has me coming undone.

I grit my teeth to hold onto some type of control. My arm wraps tightly around his waist, my other hand winds its fingers through his curly locks. I pull him upright, leaning back on my haunches, lifting him so that he's seated on my cock, his legs spread out around mine with his back against my chest. Holding him firmly against me, the sweat dripping from our bodies mixes together forming a heady intoxicating smell.

Pulling his head back I whisper in his ear, "How funny do you think your punishment is now?" I lick it for good measure.

"My intestines are still firmly in place. Maybe try a little harder." The fucker gives me a hoarse laugh, finding himself hilarious.

I lick him again, this time from the base of his neck up to his ear. "Gladly," I say, as I begin fucking him with every ounce of strength I have left in me.

My upward thrusts are getting stronger, our bodies making vulgar sounds from the force of them. My hand that was in his hair travels to his throat, constricting around it, but not so tightly that he can't breathe. His head falls back onto my shoulder, eyes rolling backwards. His hands wrap around my body grabbing whatever he can hold onto.

"Have I fucked the brat out of you yet? Do I need to spank you some more? Will that do the trick? Forget not walking tomorrow, baby. I'm going to make sure your hole misses my cock so much you'll be begging me to come destroy it again and again." I growl each word with explicit intentions.

The groan that leaves his throat is the only warning before cum erupts from his dick and onto the bed as his body clenches around me.

Did he come hands-free?

That unanswered question combined with the pulsing around my cock sends me swan diving off the edge. I thrust up fully into him once more as my cock jerks inside him, unleashing my load into the condom. My teeth find his shoulder and clamp down, stifling the feral sounds coming from deep within me. Kaden cries out in pain-laced pleasure, and then we collapse onto the mattress.

Chapter Seventeen

I MAY NEED A REPEAT

Kaden

Luke's arms are wrapped around me, both of us a puddle of sweat and cum, out of breath from the thorough fucking he just gave me. Talk about keeping his word. He's still inside me, and I want to beg for more. I'm officially addicted to all things Luke.

On the way back to his place, I promised myself this was it, to get him out of my system—nothing more. I spent the last month sulking over him. And that was only after a couple hours of conversation and a nice cock to suck. How the fuck am I supposed to walk away from him after today? And not only because he gave me the best dicking down I've ever had, but we had a good time. He's funny and sweet. The conversation was easy. Why would I even want to walk away?

You don't, Kaden. Admit it.

I don't. The question is, does he? I think Luke and I both know he's not straight. He wasn't freaked out by anything we've done, never hesitated for a second. It wasn't like when things started with Tyler. Fuck, I hate comparing him to Tyler. I hate thinking about that jerk at all.

Luke is not Tyler. I need to stop putting him in the same box that asshole created in my head. I need to give him a chance to prove I'm worrying for no reason.

Lips on the nape of my neck snap my attention back to him. His body wrapped around mine makes me feel warm and safe. I could get lost in his arms and be completely happy never leaving. Our breathing has returned to normal, and Luke's hand splayed out on my stomach brushes gently across my ill-defined abs. They're nothing like his cum gutters for sure, and forget about a six-pack, the man has craters between his eight-pack. I wanted to lick through every one of them earlier, but I was too eager to get his cock in my mouth again.

"Penny for your thoughts?" Luke whispers between kisses on my neck and shoulders.

"I may need to charge a little more. There's some interesting stuff happening up here right now." I tap my temple.

"I'm not sure if it's anything compared to mine." He huffs a half-hearted laugh.

I can't help the reaction my body has to his words. I know he felt it too when his arms tighten around me.

"Stop. It's not what you think. I promise." Luke does his best to reassure me.

"How do you know what I'm thinking?"

"Besides your body becoming stiff as a board and inhaling like it was your last breath, I know you've been worried about me being straight."

He pauses long enough for me to take in that he's read me all along.

"What I don't understand is why you're so worried. I'm obviously interested in you. I think you're interested in me too. What does it matter what adjective I used to label myself with?"

Ignoring his question, which I am for sure as hell not getting into right now, I question his original comment. "Then what were you thinking about if it wasn't that?"

"I was thinking how much I'm enjoying my cock still being inside you and wondering how I could take up residence there for the foreseeable future."

I laugh hard, and the vibrations have Luke's softening dick sliding farther out of me. "You're a fan of cock-warming, huh?"

"I am now. Your ass is like someone handing me the answer to every problem I've ever had, and making them all better," Luke whispers.

"Thank...you...I think?" I shake my head at his ridiculousness.

"Yes, it's a compliment." He laughs as he rolls over to throw the condom away, and walks off toward the bathroom.

I hear footsteps coming back shortly after, and a warm towel gently sweeps down my ass.

"Are you in any pain? I'm sorry if I was too rough."

Luke keeps surprising me. He fucks like an animal and then is sweet and takes care of me afterward. No one has ever done that for me.

"I'm okay. I'll be sore tomorrow, I'm sure, but in a good way." I smile even though he can't see it.

He pulls me so I lie on my back and continues wiping me down with another warm towel. Sitting over me on his knees, his eyes meet mine. He studies my face like it'll give him answers to questions he hasn't asked.

"What's the interesting stuff going on up there?" Luke taps on my temple this time, letting his finger slide down my face along my jawline, ending its journey in a swipe across my lips.

"Do you want the good or the bad?"

Luke's face scrunches with distaste for his options. "Let's start with the bad I guess." His forehead is wrinkled and voice uncertain.

"Earlier, your dick was distracting me from licking every inch of your abs." I give him a coy smile, to which he shakes his head and chuckles.

"I don't see that as a bad thing, but I'll happily take a raincheck on the abs-licking."

"Then you'll need to leave your pants on if I have any chance of completing my mission."

He grins, leaning down and kissing me softly. "Duly noted. If that was bad, then I'm excited to hear the good."

I hesitate, scared to death of being vulnerable with him, but I have to give him a chance. I have to give *myself* a chance to be happy.

"I'm done trying to push you away."

He doesn't respond right away, but keeps his eyes locked on mine. I wait, hoping to see something in his eyes that'll give me a clue what he's thinking.

When he finally speaks, I'm not prepared for his response. "It doesn't matter if you were done or not—I didn't plan on letting you go so easily." Luke plants a firm kiss on my lips.

Once he pulls back, he slides off the bed. Rummaging through a drawer, he grabs a pair of black boxer briefs, sliding them up those muscular legs and covering his plump ass that's screaming for me to bite it. Mental note for later. He lays a gray pair on the bed for me and walks backward toward the door. "Go take a shower while I make some food and find a movie for us to watch. I left some towels on the counter for you."

I lie there a little longer, taking a few minutes for myself to ponder everything that happened tonight. If someone had told me this morning when I woke up that by this evening I'd be lying in Luke's bed after he fucked me into oblivion, getting ready to shower and then watch a movie with him, I would have referred them to a doctor for their delusions.

Movement on the bed startles me. The massive cat strolling up the bed is a sight to behold. It has a thick orange coat and pointed ears with tufts on the tips. The fur on this cat must weigh a ton by itself. It makes its way up to my face, purring like a car muffler.

I reach out to pet it as it starts rubbing its face on my forehead. "Hey there, cutie. Aren't you the prettiest thing ever?" It plops itself on the bed, leaning against me. I don't think I've ever felt fur this soft on an animal.

"Fred, come and eat!" I hear Luke call from the kitchen, followed by the *pspspsps* sound we all summon cats with.

Fred jumps up and runs out of the room to find his meal. I chuckle at Luke naming his cat Fred, knowing damn well he named him after the goofy character in one of our mutually favorite movies.

I don't waste any more time as I hurry to take a quick shower. Loving the way Luke's body wash reminds me of him, I use a little more than necessary.

As I dry myself off and throw on his boxers, I feel comforted that he offered them.

Following the smell of bacon into the kitchen, I find Fred on a stool, staring at Luke on the opposite side of the island, where he turns to toss onions and peppers into a pan.

"Does he always watch you cook?" I ask him, walking over to Fred to give him some loving.

"Always. It's not like he's waiting for me to give him something. He doesn't like any human food. I guess he finds it interesting." Luke shrugs and rounds the corner.

His hand wraps around the nape of my neck, holding me still to pin his lips to mine. Fred must be jealous, as he headbutts my side, then Luke's a few times, until we separate and comply with his demands.

"Don't mind him. He's not used to sharing me," Luke says, returning to the stove.

I file that statement away for a later discussion. "What exactly are you making?" I'm confused as I scan the counter and stove.

"Breakfast tacos. Eggs, bacon, peppers, onions, green chilies, and cheese in tortillas. Is that okay? Anything you don't like? Allergies?" Luke rambles off, pausing preparing anything else until I answer.

"No, it sounds great. I love breakfast for dinner. I'm still hungry since we barely ate at the restaurant." I sit down next to Fred, running my fingers through his fur.

"That would be *your* fault, but I'm not complaining." Luke smiles over his shoulder.

I roll my eyes, then let them wander around his apartment since I was escorted rather quickly to his bedroom when we got here. The main room is a big open-concept layout. The kitchen, of course, is the most eye-catching area. It's only natural that Luke would need plenty of space to cook more at home.

The living room is at the far side of the space, away from the door. There's a gray sectional couch in the middle of it, surrounded by coffee and end tables, and a huge flat-screen TV on the wall.

"You can go sit in there if you want. I'll bring the food when it's ready." Luke motions toward the couch.

I walk over and plop onto the couch, turning on the TV. I scroll through the apps until I find what I'm looking for.

Fred joins me on the couch, headbutting my hand. Luke follows suit a few minutes later with two plates in hand.

"These look delicious."

We both stuff our faces, enjoying the tacos and laughing between bites at Patrick breaking down the meaning of 'wumbo.'

This is nice; easy. Like we've known each other for years. By the time we finish eating and watching a couple episodes of SpongeBob and his friends' escapades, I know it's getting late. As much as I don't want to go, I'm getting tired and have to get up early tomorrow.

"I'll help you clean up and then get going. Early riser here," I say raising my hand.

Luke glances at his watch. "Shit, it's getting late, and I still have to take a shower. I have a long day tomorrow too." Without a word, he gets up from the couch, heading toward his bedroom and coming back with my clothes and his phone in hand.

He unlocks and hands me his phone. "Number. I'm not letting you leave here without it."

"Bossy much? Geez." I pretend to be offended, though I still take his phone.

Luke brings the plates to the kitchen while I get dressed and order my Uber. He meets me at the door, Fred in tow. The demanding thing that he is, he's rubbing himself all over my legs. I bend down to pet him one more time.

"I'll talk to you soon?" Luke asks with doubt in his tone.

"Yes." I kiss him passionately to back up my answer, having to hastily pull away before lack of better judgement takes hold of me and I walk straight back to his bed.

The perma-grin that remains on my face lasts until I'm in my bed, drifting to sleep. My dreams are no longer haunted with unattainable moments with Luke.

In the week since I've seen Luke last, my days have been full of random texts from him at all hours of the day. Every morning, I wake up to 2 a.m. sleep-deprived ramblings about his day. Everything from what he had to eat, to some silly thing his business partner had said or done that day. Gabe sounds like a spirited character. The current message is a selfie of Luke in bed this morning with Fred's enormous body lying on his bare tattooed chest, face nuzzled in his neck, with the caption, "I can't breathe, send help!" My grin is back.

"Hello, earth to Kaden. You still with us?" Connor breaks my train of thought, snapping his fingers in my direction.

"Sorry, what were you saying?"

"What are you staring at on your phone that has you smiling like it's Christmas morning? Rather *who* is it, because that, my friend, is a dopey lovesick smile happening." Leave it to Connor to say exactly what's on his mind.

"It's not love, hush yourself." I hit him with a stern look in warning.

"But it is *someone*—now spill the tea." He counters with a smirk, knowing he got the response he was after. "Ender, tell him to 'fess up now, or else."

Ender is lying on the couch, arm over his face, his head on Connor's leg. "Fight your own battles, Connor," he says, intent on minding his own business. Connor jerks his leg under Ender's head in retaliation. "Asshole. If Kaden doesn't want to talk about whoever it is, then leave him alone."

Connor ignores Ender's grumpiness and widens his eyes, silently encouraging me with a dramatic headshake to tell him.

"It's Luke," I say, cringing as I wait for the lecture.

Ender is suddenly interested in the conversation, turning to me with a shocked look on his face.

Connor is of course, the first to give his opinion. "That's the guy from the bathroom at that party you went to around Christmas time, right? I thought he was straight and off-limits?"

"We've been talking."

"Kaden, that doesn't answer my question. That was not a smile from talking with someone. You fucked him, didn't you? What happened to no more straight men?"

"I didn't fuck him."

Connor sees right through me. "So, he fucked you? Don't play semantics with me."

"He's not Tyler," I reply indignantly.

"Maybe he's not, and we can't tell you what to do—"

"Don't lump me into this," Ender interrupts.

Connor rolls his eyes at him and continues, "But be careful, please. I don't want to see you get hurt again."

I respond with a nod, which seems to satisfy him.

"Fine, now let's see some pictures of this snack who's giving you those heart eyes." Connor jumps up with excitement, dropping Ender's head to the couch, and crashes down next to me on the smaller couch.

I laugh at him. "I only have a couple selfies he's sent me over the past week." I pick my phone back up and open the Photos app.

"Did he send you dick pics? Please tell me he did, and share them with your friends." Connor claps his hands together as though he's praying.

Ender chimes in again from the other couch, his arm over his face again, "Please don't."

"No, he hasn't, and I wouldn't show you even if he had."

"Joy killer. Then what *can* you show me?"

I decide to only show him this morning's pic, hoping it's enough to satisfy his nosiness.

"Oh, okay. I get it now. I couldn't turn down anything from that man, either. He's hot. I bet he has a huge dick, doesn't he? Can we share him?" Connor has no shame in asking blunt questions.

"No. Stay away from him, you man-whore." I nudge Connor off of me, smiling at his antics.

"Don't slut-shame me! When I find someone who measures up to my expectations, I'll be monogamous. I refuse to settle for the bare minimum. Until then, the world is my playground."

I can't argue with his logic. My phone chirps with a text message. I see it's from an unknown number.

Hey Kaden. It's Jackson

Lanie's boyfriend

Faith gave me your number when I was over there the other night. Hope it's okay

I wanted to take Lanie out for her birthday and then all of us meet at the Garden

Can you and your friends join us? I know Lanie would want you all there

Faith had already told me the plans, and that Jackson asked for my number. It feels weird to text him, knowing he doesn't know about Luke and me...hooking up? It feels a little more than that now, but according to Lanie, he hasn't said anything about it. I don't want to ask Luke, obviously, because it's nothing to talk about yet, and I don't want him to think he has to do anything for me.

"You guys are still coming to The Garden for Lanie's birthday, right?"

"Of course, wouldn't miss it for the world." Connor is quick to respond.

"Who'll be there?" Ender isn't as eager.

"Just us, Jackson, probably his cousin Dakota. Not sure anyone else will be there."

"Your boyfriend isn't coming?" Ender is moodier than usual today.

"He's not my boyfriend, and he hasn't said anything about it, so I assume not. Plus, he's super busy with the restaurant. I doubt he has the time."

"Fine, I'll go."

We've learned to ignore his mood swings over the years. Ender has had a rough life, albeit he's only in his late 20s. We can't fault him for having shitty parents. We've learned the difference between Ender wanting to engage with people and wanting to be alone to destress. This is one of those in-between stages where he doesn't want to be alone but would rather not converse if he doesn't have to.

> Hi Jackson! Yes, we're all going to meet up with y'all. Let me know what time you plan on getting there with Lanie.

> That's great. Thanks, and can't wait to meet you officially *smiley face emoji*

Lanie and Jackson have been stuck together like glue, so much so that she hasn't hung out with any of us, except Faith by default because they live together. I don't blame her though. She's hopelessly in love already. I'm not even in love with Luke, and I want to spend all my time with him if it wasn't for the restaurant keeping him so busy.

Just one more month...

Chapter Eighteen

He Knows How To Make Me Smile

Luke

I haven't seen Kaden in almost three weeks, and it keeps getting harder. I've been working every day of the week, getting the final details ready for the opening next month. Most nights I'm not walking through my door until after midnight. I would've asked Kaden to come over some nights, but knowing I wouldn't be able to keep my hands off him, is a sure-fire way to not get any sleep. I'm trying to hold out until Lanie's birthday, knowing I'll see him then, but with him sending me selfies like the one I'm staring at, I don't know how much longer I'll last. This one is of him in bed last night, shirtless, on his side, half asleep and looking at the camera. The caption, "This could be your view right now if you were here." He has no idea how much I wish I were there.

"Stop making googly eyes at your boyfriend's sexting pics," Gabe says over my shoulder, standing where I'm seated at the bar.

I lay my phone face down on the bar next to the paperwork I was supposed to be working on. "It wasn't a sexting pic, you dickhead."

Gabe takes the seat next to me. "So, you haven't sexted after not seeing each other for three weeks? What the fuck, man? You like torturing yourself? Send him a fucking dick pic—I guarantee he sends one back." He wiggles his brows and gives me a shit-eating grin.

"You know, just because you like unsolicited dick pics, doesn't mean everyone does, right?"

"Fine, tell him to send *me* the dick pics, and I'll make good use of them."

"Stay away from Kaden's dick, or you'll have to find a new best friend, along with some new teeth."

"Ooooohhhhh, getting possessive already. I can't wait to meet him on your birthday. This is going to be so much fun."

I invited Gabe to Lanie's and my birthday hangout at The Garden. I told Jackson not to make a big deal about it being my birthday too. Well, my birthday is the day after Lanie's, on March 4th, but Jackson said he's starting a new tradition for us to celebrate our birthdays together, since he plans on marrying her. My jaw dropped to the floor when he said that to me. He's known the girl for two months, and he thinks he's ready to marry her. I'm trying to convince myself this is simply another one of Jackson's impulsive moments. Only time will tell, so I'll entertain his whole shared birthday party tradition. As of now, he hasn't told anyone it's my birthday, or I imagine Kaden would have said something already.

"Gabe, don't fuck with me around Kaden. I won't be held responsible for what happens."

"Man, chill. I'm not going to hit on your guy." He goes quiet for a minute while I get back to the papers in front of me.

"You really like him, don't you?" He sounds genuinely interested.

"Yeah, I do. It's easy with us. We haven't technically spent a lot of time together, but between texts and phone calls, I've gotten to know a lot about him. He's funny and witty. He's sexy as hell despite not trying to be. We like the same foods and movies, even sports. I mean, how many gay guys like hockey, besides you of course?"

"Uh Luke, have you actually seen how hot hockey players are? Trust me, plenty of us watch hockey, especially the warmups." He fans himself, as if he's overheating just thinking about it.

I shake my head at him. "Yeah, I guess some of them are kind of good looking."

"Yep, you got it bad." Gabe slaps my shoulder and saunters off toward the kitchen.

"Hey," I call after him, and he turns to listen. "Do you think you can stick around for the servers' training sessions with Jessica on Saturday? I want to take the day off."

"Of course. Have a good time, buddy." Gabe nods with a knowing grin and turns back onto his path.

I text Kaden as soon as Gabe is out of sight.

> Hey sexy. I cleared my schedule for Saturday.

> Do you want to join me and veg out on the couch, watching mindless shows all day with my arms wrapped around you?

> Please say yes so I don't have to come kidnap you.

He reads it as soon as it's delivered. Dots pop up right away. I hope that's a good sign.

> As much as I want to, I have plans this weekend already. Ender has been really down lately, and Connor saw his favorite band is playing in Atlanta this weekend.

> He got lucky and was able to get us some tickets.

> So, we made it a weekend trip. We're leaving tomorrow and coming back on Sunday.

My stomach cramps up. Why did I wait until the last minute? Of course he has plans. What do I expect—him to wait at home for me?

> Okay, no problem. I'll try and make some time next week. Have fun and stay out of trouble *winky face emoji*

Well, there goes that idea. Guess I'll be cuddling with Fred all day. My phone chirps again.

> Can I make it up to you?

I smile, knowing he wants to see me, too.

> How?

I stare at my phone, burning a hole through it waiting for his response. There aren't any dots popping up, either. A few minutes pass, and still nothing. I sigh and set the phone back down on the bar.

I continue with my paperwork, trying not to obsess over why he didn't respond. My phone finally chirps again. When I unlock the screen and see what's in the chat from Kaden, my heart rate spikes and my cock swells to life.

I quickly turn to make sure no one is around, then pick my phone back up. The selfie Kaden sent, his phone must have been propped up and set on a timer because both his hands are very occupied. He's lying on his back in bed, completely nude.. One hand is teasing his nipple while the other is wrapped around his hard cock, thumb over his slit. His head is on his pillow, tilted toward the camera, allowing me to see his hooded gaze and parted lips, tongue peeking out ever so slightly between them.

I take a few deep breaths and palm the bulge trying to spring free from my jeans. I save the pic to enjoy later, and start typing a response.

> I'm not sure if you're trying to make it up to me or kill me right now. *big eyes emoji* *eggplant emoji* *hot face emoji*

> If I was trying to kill you I would have sent you a video.

I start to type out a typical smartass reply when I hear the *swoosh* sound of an incoming message, and a video pops up in the chat.

Fuck. Me.

Don't hit play. Don't hit play. Don't hit play.

I hit play and hold the phone to my chest, obstructing anyone else's view. I lower the volume all the way as soon as I hear his heavy panting.

Kaden touching himself has to be the sexiest thing I've ever seen. His hand that was pinching his nipple in the picture is now fondling his balls while he fucks his fist with enthusiasm. The veins in his neck and forearms are standing out enticingly against his skin.

My cock is aching in my jeans, and, glancing around to make sure nobody comes into the room, I push the heel of my hand down to try to relieve some of the pressure. Thankfully, it's getting late, and only a few of the kitchen staff are still here, working with Gabe. I turn back to my phone in time to see Kaden shoot his load all over himself.

Thinking the video was ending, I go to close it, stopping when Kaden swipes his fingers across his stomach. He brings them to his lips, smearing his cum over them, then licking it up.

Just call a fucking hearse for me now.

I don't think I've ever walked so fast in my life, taking a direct path to the back office Gabe and I share. Locking the door behind me, I prop up the phone in front of the guest chair on the desk and press play again. I undo my jeans and rip my cock out of its jail cell, giving it the room it desperately needs, and jerk myself until I come in tandem with Kaden this time. A low growl leaves my throat as I watch his tongue swipe up his...*my*...cum from his lips.

I'm attempting to restore my breathing back to normal when a knock on the door startles me.

"Hey asshole, open up," Gabe's voice demands from the other side of it.

"One sec," I rush to answer, grabbing some tissues from the box on the desk. I was in such a hurry to relieve the ache in my balls that I didn't think about preparing for the mess I was about to make. I wipe myself up as much as I can and throw the tissues in the basket next to the desk. Shoving my dick back in my pants, I walk to the door, just as Gabe starts to knock louder this time.

"Geez I'm coming. What's your deal, man?" I respond, exasperated, opening the door for him.

Gabe looks at me wide-eyed, an evil smirk plastered on his face. His gaze falls from my face to my shirt hem and back up. "I guess the dick pic worked, huh?" The fucker laughs, but then his eyes get caught on something behind me.

I turn to see what he's staring at. "Shit." I scramble to the desk and grab my phone, shoving it in my pants pocket. The fucking video ended, going back to the beginning, waiting to be played again with Kaden's fisted cock in full view.

Looking back towards Gabe, his shocked expression turns to elation. "Video, even better. You might want to take the time to remove your shirt next time, though." He laughs again, pointing to my shirt, where I've made a mess of myself.

"Fuck you, asshole. Out!" I chuckle, pushing him fully out the door, slamming it behind him. His boisterous laugh echoes down the hall as he retreats.

My phone chirps, and I realize I never responded to the video.

> Did I really kill you?

> I'm alive, barely. Had to find some privacy and made a mess of myself. Thanks for the break but when I finally get to see you again, your ass will have my handprints burned into it by the time I'm finished with you.

> Don't threaten me with a good time. Guess you'll have to take a day off and prove it to me. *face with stuck out tongue and closed eyes emoji*

In the middle of responding to his continued bratty behavior, my phone rings. Kaden's number appears on the screen.

"Hey." My voice is barely audible when I answer the call, relaxing back in the chair behind the desk.

"Hey, back." Kaden sounds tired. "Sorry you made a mess of your-self."

"No, you're not, but nice try. Nothing to be sorry about anyway. It was a nice present." I smile as if he can see it.

"Yeah? Am I forgiven for turning you down for the weekend plans?"

"It's fine. It's my fault for not trying to make plans sooner. I've been so busy I haven't had much time to breathe, much less have a personal life." I sigh, stretching as if even talking about it is exhausting.

"Is that why Fred isn't used to sharing you?"

"Hmmm, you were paying attention."

"Always."

Hearing his voice alone relaxes me. I want more.

"Would it be crazy for me to tell you how much I want to come see you right now?"

"No, because I think I want you here more. Maybe we're both crazy."

"Will you be awake in half an hour?" I silently pray he says yes.

"I couldn't fall asleep now if my life depended on it." Kaden's promise lights a fire in me.

"See you soon, Angel."

"See you soon. Drive safely."

I gather my keys and paperwork I'll need to work on at home, and head out the door. I stop by the kitchen to check on Gabe and one of the managers still here with him.

"Hey, you okay here? Alright if I leave? I don't need Saturday off anymore." I add the latter part, so he doesn't think Kaden being in my life is going to interfere with my responsibilities as his business partner.

"Yes. Go spend time with your guy. Have some kind of personal life for once." Gabe knows how solitary I've been for years. He's tried really hard to make me see I could have a personal life while pursuing my dream. I'm glad I never let him convince me—I wouldn't have met Kaden if he had.

I make it to Kaden's apartment a little after 11 p.m. and I'm hoping he hasn't fallen asleep. I know he gets up early to go running every day, so he has an early bedtime. I knock lightly on his door, and wait. When it opens, it feels like the loaded weight I've been carrying on my shoulders suddenly disappears. Kaden answers the door, sleepy-eyed in a pair of baggy bed shorts and nothing else.

He doesn't even wait for me to come in, just steps into me, wrapping his arms around my neck and nuzzling into the crook. I follow his lead, letting him fall into my arms, inhaling his scent and kissing him on the head.

"You look really tired. Let's get you to bed." He gives me the cutest little whine.

I start walking forward with him still in my arms. It winds up being too awkward with him walking backward while half asleep, so I do the next best thing, grabbing him by his ass and lifting him up to carry him. He instinctively wraps his legs around me, then Kaden's head falls to my shoulder, his lips planting a kiss at the base of my neck. It's still not easy carrying him with Kaden being a fairly big guy and me not knowing where his bedroom is, but I manage to get us there in one piece.

I tap his ass, signaling him to release his grip around me so I can set him down on the bed. He doesn't get the hint. I kneel on the bed, slowly lowering us both together, sliding the covers away. Once we're both lying down safely, I kick my shoes off and pull the covers back over us.

Kaden finally releases his grip around my waist, his leg probably uncomfortable underneath my side. I roll to my back and pull him in tight against my side, his head resting on my shoulder, arm and leg slung over my body.

Like magic, all the tension and stress in my mind and body fall away. Feeling the warmth of his body through my clothes and the soft sounds of his breathing by my ear relaxes me like nothing I've ever experienced. My last thought as I drift off to sleep?

Peaceful.

Chapter Nineteen

I've Never Been So Happy to be Dirty

Kaden

I wake up to the sun shining through the gaps in the curtains, my bed-side lamp still on, and Luke fully clothed with me wrapped around him like a koala. I don't want to move, and not because I don't want to wake him. This feels good...*right*.

I don't even remember him getting here last night. I was nodding off on the couch waiting for him, then I vaguely remember being carried to the bedroom. The thought of what that must have looked like, my six-foot frame wrapped around him as he walked around looking for my bedroom. An amused snort escapes me, and Luke stirs.

"What's so funny this early in the morning," he mumbles, squeezing my ass with the hand that's behind me while he rubs his eyes with the other.

He kisses my head and pulls me on top of him. I straddle him, splaying my hands across his chest and resting my chin on them to look up at him.

"Why are you still in all your clothes?"

"Someone was stuck to my body like glue, making it impossible to take them off," Luke says, rubbing his thumb across my lower lip. I take it in my mouth, sucking and twirling my tongue around it before releasing it. His pupils dilate at the motion.

"That kind of sounds like a complaint, Mr. Stonewood."

"It was most definitely not a complaint. I haven't slept that well in years. And it's 'Mr. Snugglebug' to you. I think I proved deserving of the name after last night." He laughs at himself.

"I guess so." I shrug my shoulders.

"You guess so, huh? Maybe we should stay in bed all day so I can convince you a little more." He reaches up and softly kisses my forehead.

Why does that make me swoon a little harder?

"Ugh, don't tempt me. My schedule is full today, and we leave for Atlanta around six." I suddenly regret making plans, lying here in Luke's arms and knowing this could have been my Saturday.

"I have shit to do today, too. I suppose I can convince you another night when you get back from your weekend getaway with the guys." Luke's arms tighten around me as he flips us so I'm under him.

He tenderly kisses me all over my shoulders, neck, and face. I lean my head back farther on the pillow, giving him more skin to place his lips on. Gently thrusting forward, his hardened dick finds mine in the same state through our clothes. I pull him into me harder by his ass, spreading my legs wider to make more room for him.

"If you don't stop, neither of us is going to make it out the door today." I internally curse at myself for having to say the words.

He sighs and rests his forehead on my chest. I run my fingers through his hair, massaging his scalp, and he groans in appreciation.

"Can we at least take a shower before I leave? I want to hold onto you a little longer."

How could I say no to that? "*Just* holding. No funny business, Snugglebug." He laughs at my use of his self-proclaimed pet name.

"Deal. Let's go." He rises from the bed, bringing me with him, our fingers entwined.

I turn the water to the hot side, and within a minute, the steam envelops us as I watch Luke strip down. With his back to me, he bends down to remove his jeans and boxers around his feet, that plump ass bare for the taking. I can't resist the temptation—I lean over and take a quick bite of it.

"What the f—*oowww*," Luke screeches, jumping forward against the counter.

"Sorry, couldn't help myself. I've been wanting to do that for a long time." I laugh, turning around to hop in the shower.

Luke follows me, closing the door behind him, grabbing my hands, and pulling my arms above my head as he pins me to the wall. The tiles are cool against my face, and I shut my eyes and relish in the sensations igniting over me all at once. His naked body pressing firmly against mine, and his long, stiff cock sitting perfectly between my ass cheeks.

I feel his breath in my ear, lips caressing my lobe. "You said no funny business. Does this feel funny to you?" His raspy tone is followed by a forceful thrust, pushing me harder against the tiles, my dick suffering the consequences of my actions.

"Definitely not funny. I suppose it's not breaking the rules then." Breathless and horny, I push my ass back into his cock.

One of Luke's hands loosens around mine and travels slowly down my arms, rounding my chest and pulling me away from the wall enough for his hand to continue its path. His tongue flicks out before he sucks my neck and shoulder. His hand meets its destination, cocooning my cock, gently stroking me. I allow my head to fall back onto his shoulder with a groan.

The contact takes my breath away. Feeling his hand on me for the first time sends every sensory receptor in my body into overdrive. His hand closes firmly around me as his strokes speed up. I move my free hand down behind me, fisting his cock. I spread my legs as I position him between my thighs, and squeeze.

Our moans echo against the shower walls. I reach for the body wash, pushing the bottle against his arm. "Pour some on yourself," I unashamedly beg him.

He pulls back and I turn to see him grabbing the bottle, dumping an obscene amount into his shaking hand. I catch my breath, leaning on a forearm against the wall while he lathers himself up and shoves his cock back between my legs. As I clench my thighs together, he begins thrusting, his gel-slicked hand surrounding my cock again. His other hand is on my stomach, bracing me against he thrusts in time with his strokes, both increasing in pace.

Luke's sputtering obscenities, interjected between compliments on the sounds coming out of my mouth and how stunning I am when he's fucking me, sends me spiraling into ecstasy.

"Come with me. Can you come for me?" Luke requests breathlessly.

"Yes. Please, now. I can't..." Flashes of light form behind my eyelids as I try to finish the thought, and my aching balls tighten. Then my release is covering his hand and the wall.

Luke's cock pulses between my thighs, and he sinks his teeth into my shoulder, his massive body jerking as his cum coats my inner thighs, animalistic growls rising from deep within him.

We both fall forward, his body crushing mine into the wall. As we attempt to breathe like humans once again, Luke starts to laugh.

"What's so funny?" I ask, turning around, still caged in by this magnificent specimen of a man.

"I can't believe I've had almost fifteen years of sexual experiences and never knew what was missing until I met you." He seems surprised.

I smile with him. "I'm glad I could be the one to show you what you've been missing."

"Me too." His lips meet mine in a ravaging battle for control, and my own become pliant against his demands.

I've lost any fight to resist this man. He has me at his mercy.

At least we agree on something.

Chapter Twenty

Happy Birthday to Us

Luke

After Thursday night, I've counted down the minutes to tonight, when I get to see Kaden again. The complete 180 I've done in the relationship department in a few months has shocked me, to say the least. I'm approaching The Garden, very excited to see the surprise on his face when I show up. He texted me around eight to tell me he arrived, and that he'll talk to me later when he gets home. Dakota and Gabe have already texted and are on their way, too. I wanted to get here ahead of Dakota and Jackson so I can feel Kaden out before we get thrown into answering a hundred questions about us. It's not that I don't want them to know about Kaden and me seeing each other, but we haven't spoken about telling anyone besides his friends and Gabe. I don't want to assume anything.

I walk into the bar, looking around for him, and spot him on one of the couches with Faith and a couple guys. I recognize them from the pictures Kaden posted on his social media account over the weekend from their trip to Atlanta.

I can't say I wasn't a little jealous of them. Especially the one with blond shaggy hair and a septum piercing. Ender is his name, according to the tag on a picture of his arms wrapped around Kaden, kissing him on the cheek during the concert. In another picture of the three of them, he's blatantly staring at Kaden with too much affection for my liking. I love Gabe like a brother, but I don't look at him like Ender was looking at Kaden. I shove those thoughts down as I approach the group.

"Hey there," I say, leaning down behind Kaden, brushing his ear with my lips.

He startles, turning around to look up at me.

"Holy shit, you scared me." He jumps up, greeting me with a smile. "What are you doing here? You didn't tell me you were coming tonight."

"I wanted to surprise you." My hands, as if on autopilot, latch onto his hips, pulling him in close as I place my lips on his forehead in a soft kiss.

"Ummmm what's going on here?" Faith interrupts our embrace. I forgot she was here for a second.

"Faith, you remember Luke. From the Christmas party we went to?" Kaden ignores her question.

"Of course I do. How could I forget Jackson's hot as fuck older brother? My question is how did this happen?" She motions her hand between Kaden and me. I guess he hasn't told her anything.

"Story for another time." Kaden brushes the topic off and introduces me to his other friends. "Guys, this is Luke. That's Ender and Connor," he says, pointing from one to the other.

Ender, not looking happy to see me, gives me a slight wave and goes back to drinking his beer. I give him a "hey" and a nod.

Connor stands from his seat, extending his hand, and I mirror his action. "Nice to finally meet you." Then he cups his hand to the side of his mouth, leaning towards Kaden, and says, "He's hotter in person," loud enough for all to hear.

Kaden and I laugh in sync at Connor. He reminds me of Gabe. The two of them together should be a fun time.

As if summoned, Gabe strolls up behind me and clasps my shoulder. "What's so funny there, brother?"

"I was telling Kaden how hot Luke is—seems it runs in the family." Connor reaches his hand out to Gabe. "Connor. Nice to meet you, gorgeous."

"Gabe, likewise." Gabe chuckles and gives him a wink. They're very much alike.

"Connor, can you stop hitting on everyone for, I don't know, thirty minutes, maybe? Is that possible?" Kaden jokes.

"Timer starts now, then all bets are off." Connor checks his watch. We all share a laugh, except Ender. Surprisingly, his sullen expression has changed, though, and his eyes track Gabe leaving the group instead. Interesting.

"I'm going to grab a beer. You want one?" Gabe asks as he walks toward the bar.

"Yeah, thanks," I call after him, then take a seat with Kaden on the empty couch, laying my arm across the back behind his shoulders.

"Jackson texted. They're on their way," Faith announces, face in her phone as Dakota arrives.

"What's up, guys? Cousin, you decided to join the land of the living." He chuckles, taking a seat next to Faith and staring at my arm around Kaden.

Faith scoots away from Dakota so their legs are no longer touching. Dakota notices. "Hi, Faith."

She smiles with pursed lips, narrowing her eyes in what seems like disdain. Poor guy has no shot with her, but I commend his persistence.

He moves on to introducing himself to Connor and Ender. Connor conspicuously checks his watch and looks at Kaden, who shakes his head at him. I decide I really like Connor. I can see why Kaden is friends with him. His antics should make for a good time tonight.

Gabe returns with my beer in hand and glances toward Ender, noticing him for the first time. Gabe moves with purpose, sitting right next to him on the third couch in the space we've taken over.

Soon, the conversation picks up as everyone starts getting to know each other. My hand behind Kaden, having a mind of its own apparently, moves around the nape of his neck, thumb drawing circles on his warm skin. He leans into it, giving me that comforting feeling that he wants the connection as much as I do.

"Oh, my Goddesses! What are you all doing here?" Lanie screeches from behind us. As soon as I turn, I see Jackson's eyes on my hand. Kaden jumps up to give his sister a hug, then, distracting Jackson.

Lanie introduces Jackson to Kaden, formally. Jackson makes his way to me as Lanie goes around the group, handing out more hugs and cheek kisses.

"Happy birthday, brother." My eyes flash to Kaden as his find mine. The look on his face tells me I might be in trouble.

"Thanks, man. Here to celebrate hers, though, not mine." He nods in understanding before our typical greeting of clasped hands and pats on the back.

Lanie joins us, giving me the strongest hug imaginable from such a tiny woman, and a look that conveys she knows everything I thought she didn't. "Nice to finally meet you, Luke."

"You too, Lanie. Happy Birthday." Jackson hugs her from behind, pulling her down on the fourth couch, and she giggles as they complete the gathering of new friends.

"Time's up!" Connor announces, "How dare your family have genes to pass on like this? Is everyone in your family beyond fuckable? Geez." He stares in amazement, his eyes moving from Jackson, to me, to Dakota. He leans around Ender to question Gabe. "Are you really in the family? Because those genes spread to you too."

"For Christ's sake, Connor, will you control your hormones tonight, please?" Ender speaks up finally.

"Hush yourself. Let me ogle them in peace." They begin to bicker like siblings, the rest of us laughing at them.

We resume conversation like we're all old friends. Our animated group is all that exists around us, and my, for reasons I don't care to think about right now. I want to focus on the here and now.

We share stories, laughing at each other's mishaps and the shenanigans we got up to as teenagers. Gabe, Kaden, Ender, and I wind up debating whose hockey team is heading toward the finals. Gabe, being a Canadiens' fan, and Ender, a Bruins' fan, known rival teams, get into a petty argument that looks more like foreplay if I'm being honest.

Watching their banter, I look over at Kaden, and my heart stutters seeing the vibrant smile across his face from spending time with friends. He catches me staring at him and smiles coyly.

I lean into his ear and whisper, "Come get another drink with me." He nods as I get up and extend my hand to help him off the couch, and I see Jackson's eyes on us in my periphery. I'm sure I'll be answering some of his questions later.

I lead Kaden to the bar. Making space for him next to me, we face each other. Our eyes meet, and I immediately feel his seductive gaze pull me into his orbit. Taking hold of the back of his neck, I follow the invisible threads that bind us, and connect his lips to mine.

The kiss is gentle, and we savor it before remembering we're in public. I pull away and see the bartender glance our way, nodding to acknowledge him.

"Hey guys, what can I get you?" He's tall and covered in tattoos with a neatly cared-for beard.

I order our beers while Kaden's hand finds its way under the hem of my shirt, latching onto my side above the waistline of my jeans. When I turn back to face him, there's heat behind his eyes.

"You need to control those eyes of yours, otherwise I'll be dragging you out of here like a caveman and fucking you bare over the hood of my truck."

His Adam's apple bobs as he swallows hard, no doubt visualizing the scene I created for him.

Kaden doesn't get a chance to respond because Faith joins us. "Please, someone get me a dozen shots of Tequila so I can make it through the rest of the night." Her eyes bounce from Kaden to me, neither of us looking away from each other.

"Jesus Christ, you two need to stop eye-fucking each other over here before the whole bar catches the contagion and starts a massive orgy."

Faith's raunchy comment catches both of our attention.

"Why are you so on edge, Faith?" Kaden asks.

"Nothing, it's not important. Can you order me a couple shots, please?"

I oblige when the bartender comes back with our beers. I see Dakota at the other end of the bar, looking our way, over the shoulder of the other bartender.

Kaden and Faith chat while we wait for her shots. She downs them back-to-back when they arrive.

Dakota enters our mini circle with two drinks, and offers one to Faith. "I got you a drink. I asked for something fruity. Thought you would like it."

Faith looks down at the open-cupped drink, then back up to Dakota. "Did you roofie this?"

Dakota's shocked expression matches both mine and Kaden's. He's stunned into silence, retreating with both drinks still in hand.

"Faith, what the fuck?" Kaden says to her.

"What? He keeps hovering over me. What am I supposed to think?"

"I can assure you, Faith, Dakota would never roofie you. He's the most harmless person I've ever met. And I'm not saying that because he's family," I say to her.

She looks from me to Kaden and then away, staring off into seemingly nowhere.

Kaden shakes his head, letting me know it's not something to get into right now.

Dakota returns with a sealed bottle of water, handing it to Faith with an apologetic look. She takes it without opposition. Dakota walks away without a word, returning to the couches with our friends.

"I'm going back over there. I'll see you in a few." I kiss Kaden's cheek and leave to check on Dakota.

These two have the weirdest encounters. It's confusing as hell, but hopefully Kaden can figure out what's bothering Faith.

I miss him already.

Chapter Twenty-One

I Was Tired. That's My Story and I'm Sticking to It

Kaden

Once Luke is out of earshot, I turn to Faith with concern. "Faith, what's going on?"

"Nothing, Dakota is too nice. Clingy. I can't deal with it right now," she rattles off, waving down the bartender again. "You're doing shots with me. You can't make me drink alone."

She orders a quad of tequila shots, not even giving me a choice. I'd do anything for Faith, and she seems to really need someone right now, so of course I slam both shots back with her and chase them with my beer.

We talk for a little while longer, both singing to a random song the DJ played at one point. Then we order another round of shots. Her bad mood seemingly gone makes me happy, until she takes her phone from her back pocket, having received a text message. She reads it, and frustration bleeds from her as she puts it back in her pocket.

"I'm running to the restroom. I'll meet you back over there." She walks away without another word.

I think Lanie and I are going to need some alone time with Faith to figure out what's going on with her. She's been acting weird lately. The way she's treating Dakota is strange, when he's been nothing but nice to her the couple times they've met.

As I'm walking back to the little corner we've taken over, I feel the effects of the shots and more than a few beers I've had. I think I should have eaten something more substantial than a few French fries before coming here.

I sit down next to Luke, who's talking with Dakota on his other side. Jackson and Lanie are chatting with Connor, and Gabe and Ender seem to be lost in their own conversation.

Luke's hand impulsively lands on my thigh, squeezing it, sending shivers through my body. I drop my head onto his shoulder, needing to be as close as our surroundings allow us. When Dakota gets up from the couch and walks toward the restrooms, Luke turns his attention on me.

"You having a good time?" he asks, nuzzling my head.

"Yes. This is nice." I stifle a yawn, the alcohol making me sleepier than I already am at this time of night. "Hey, why didn't you tell me it was your birthday?"

"Because it's not." He says.

I try to make sense between what Luke said, and Jackson saying it was his birthday earlier. The grin tells me all I need to know. "Tomorrow is my birthday."

"Ha ha, very funny. Two strikes against you now." He can't claim I didn't warn him.

"Two?"

"Avoiding telling me, and being a smartass about it."

"I wasn't avoiding it for any reason other than—it's just another day, and I'd rather tonight be for Lanie."

Why does he have to be so sweet?

Luke checks his watch. "It's almost midnight. You have work tomorrow, right?"

Oh, it's later than I thought. "No, I asked Kelsey on Friday to reschedule all tomorrow's appointments. I knew after the weekend away and tonight, I'd need some rest."

He looks confused, then says, "How many beers have you had?" Luke laughs as he asks the question.

"I don't know, a few? Faith also made me do some shots with her. Earlier, Jackson had me doing shots with Lanie. I lost count. Why?"

"You might be a little drunk, Angel." He teases, raising my chin with his free hand and capturing my lips with his. I can't process what he means when he's distracting me with his soft lips and snaking tongue.

"Get a room!" Connor has decided he's the PDA police tonight.

I groan in annoyance when Luke pulls away, laughing at Connor.

"That's our cue. See you guys later." Luke stands, holding his hand out for me to grasp.

We make our rounds of goodbyes, and when we walk toward the door, Luke waves to our new bartender friend.

When we get to his Jeep, he opens the door for me, a hint of laughter under his breath. "You're even more adorable when you're drunk, if that's possible."

"I'm not drunk. I'm tired," I huff as he buckles my seatbelt for me. I take the opportunity to palm the bulge in his jeans and give it a hard squeeze. He gives me a stern look. "What?" I innocently bat my eyelashes at him.

"Behave yourself." Luke orders, kissing me and closing my door.

The drive to wherever we're going is quiet, aside from the faint sound of music Luke put on. My wandering hand keeps getting snagged and put back where it started on the top of his thigh. I give up the fight and relax with my head against the window.

When I open my eyes, we're parked outside Luke's building, and the back of his fingers brushing along my cheeks. Once he sees I'm awake, he gets out and opens my door for me.

Luke guides me up to his apartment and straight to his bedroom. I hear Fred screaming for attention as he undresses me down to my boxers and coaxes me into bed. When he goes to walk away, I stop him, latching onto his hand and attempting to pull him onto the bed with me.

"I'm just going to get some water for us. I'll be right back." I let go and get comfortable under the covers, feeling the bed dip as Fred snuggles up behind me.

I hear Luke come back into the room, getting ready to join me. As soon as he slips under the comforter with me, our bodies join together in the middle as I wrap myself around him. "Happy Birthday, Luke. I hope you had a good night."

"Thank you. Being with you here makes it a hundred times better than any other birthday." His lips brush my forehead, and I hear myself mumble something as I drift off to sleep. Luke's arms closing tighter around me is the last thing I remember.

Chapter Twenty-Two

THREE SIMPLE WORDS

Luke

*Y*ou're not him.

How could three words Kaden uttered in a sleep haze send me spiraling? "You're not him." I'm not who? And is that a good thing or a bad thing? Is he disappointed I'm not him? Is he hung up on someone, and I missed the signs? I don't think I misread what this is between us, but even so, I need answers. How do I even approach this, though? And will he tell me the truth?

Of course he will. When has he ever lied to me?

With too many ominous thoughts running through my head all night, I haven't slept a wink. I just lay there, holding him as tight as I could, wondering when it'll be the last time that I can. When will he stop being *mine*? Was he ever really mine? How and when did I become dependent on his presence in my life?

I want to scream in frustration, but I don't want to wake him. I want to stay like this for as long as possible.

Fred senses my unease and comes to lie down next to my head, nudging my face with his nose. He really does know when I need his support.

It's a little past six when Kaden starts to wake. He groans as if in pain.

"Good morning. How're you feeling?" I try to act normal.

"Like I got hit by a freight train. I didn't think I drank enough to feel this bad. Did I pass out on you last night?"

"I don't know about that. You did have four or five beers and at least half a dozen shots with Lanie and Faith. I think Connor may have snuck you one or two as well. Seems like enough to get you more than a little tipsy," I tease. "And yeah, my excellent snuggling skills had you asleep in no time." I'm dying inside to ask him who 'him' is.

"I have to admit, you are a pretty good Snugglebug. One of the best, maybe."

"Am I the only one?" I can't resist the opening he left me.

Kaden pulls back and looks at me like I grew five heads all of a sudden. "What do you mean?"

I sigh deeply and face this head-on. "Last night before you fell asleep, you said, 'You're not him.' Who's 'him'?"

Kaden's face goes pale as he looks away from me, and my heart drops.

"It's not what you think."

"Then what is it?"

He pulls his legs under him, sitting crisscross applesauce, facing toward me. I follow suit and sit up. "Let me start by saying I feel really bad for doing this, and it won't ever happen again." Taking a deep breath, he continues, "I've been comparing you to my sort-of ex since we met."

My turn to take a deep breath, dropping my eyes to my hands in my lap.

"Hear me out."

I nod, waiting to hear the rest. I'm doing my best not to react poorly, though my stomach is in knots.

"We met at the beginning of our second year of dental school. We had a lot in common, and we had the same study habits, so it was an easy friendship. Then my feelings grew into something more. Typical gay-guy-falls-for-his-straight-friend sad story, right?" He huffs, and I can't help but copy him.

"Toward the end of that school year, things started to change. Tyler was staring longer, friendly touches on a hand or arm turned into more, hugs lasted longer. One thing led to another, and it turned into a full-blown relationship. The only problem was, Tyler would never admit it to anyone. Behind closed doors we were like any other couple. In public, we were two guy friends—studying, hanging out, doing normal day-to-day things. That lasted almost two years."

"I don't know why I put up with it for so long." He pauses, contemplating his words. "Scratch that, I do know why. Because Tyler kept reassuring me that he loved me, and it wouldn't be forever. He wanted to get through school, and then we could be together out in the open. He always came up with what felt at the time like logical reasons why it had to be that way. He was my first boyfriend, believe it or not. I didn't see the red flags staring me in the face. Like they say, love is blind, so I believed him."

"You were in love with him?" I hesitate asking, not knowing if I really want to hear the answer.

"Yeah, well, at least I thought it was love. I guess."

"Why did it end?"

"A month before graduation, Tyler was acting weird, being crude and short whenever we spoke. Then he started backpedaling, saying he couldn't worry about being in a relationship right now. I was too distracting. He needed to focus on his INBDE exams and his career. Then he could think about settling down once he was established. For added effect, his last words to me were, 'You know I'm not gay, so I don't know why this is a surprise to you' in a text message, like he wanted to rub salt in my wounds. I haven't heard from him since."

"And that's why you were pushing me away when we first met. I was straight, like him, and that's a bad thing."

123

"I swore off all straight men after Tyler. In hindsight, it wasn't fair to you. I shouldn't have compared you, or anyone for that matter, to him. Just because one guy is an asshole, doesn't mean they'll all be like him."

We sit in silence for a moment. I can see he's deep in thought, though.

"Is that everything? Seems like there's more to the story."

He huffs out an annoyed laugh. "Engagement photos with his high school sweetheart showed up all over his social media accounts a couple months after graduation—'Meant to be' and 'Soulmates' captions and all. Talk about kicking someone when they're down." Kaden shakes his head in disbelief. I can't say I blame him. Tyler sounds like a fucking dick, and I'd like to beat his ass for hurting Kaden like that.

"It fucked with my head. I'd already withdrawn from almost everything in my life after the breakup. I was barely getting through the final month of the semester—thankfully, I passed all my exams. When I found the posts of his engagement, it only got worse. If it hadn't been for me joining my aunt at her practice, I probably wouldn't have found a job anytime soon."

My loathing for Tyler grows exponentially the more Kaden talks. I reach out, taking his hand in mine. He smiles at the connection.

"Honestly, Ender was the one to get me out of my funk. He was there every day, comforting me."

And that explains a lot. I can see where this is going already.

"While I'm baring my soul to you, I might as well tell you everything. Ender and I were together. Well, not together as in dating, but in the intimate sense." He looks nervously at me, waiting to see my reaction.

As much as I want to be jealous or upset that he hadn't told me already, I can't. It sounds like Ender was there for him in a time of need. I can respect that.

I nod, acknowledging his confession, and squeeze his hand, letting him know it's not a big deal to me.

"It's not happening anymore, right?" I ask, already knowing the answer at this point, I think.

"No. Definitely not. It only lasted a few months. I'm not sure how it ended, but we went back to being friends like it never happened."

"I'm not so sure he feels the same way."

Kaden looks confused.

"He looks at you like you hung the moon. And is obviously very standoffish with me."

"That's how Ender usually is. He hasn't had the easiest life. Loser, drug addict parents. Always sketchy people in their house. Never any food. We all met in middle school. Ender spent most of his time at either mine or Connor's house. He wound up moving in with Connor's family the summer before junior year of high school. His parents didn't even notice he was gone. Connor's parents couldn't stand seeing Ender suffer the consequences of his parents' actions any longer. He started doing well in school. Was able to get some help with college funding. It turned out for the best for him. He still gets in his head and depressed pretty often. We've learned to recognize when it's coming, and to be there for him until it passes."

Now I feel bad for judging him without knowing anything about him.

"I'm glad you had him to be there for you, and you for him. I can see why you guys are all close now."

"Yeah, my inner circle is strong." He laughs.

"I hope I can be considered in that circle now." I hold my breath for the answer.

"Not a chance," Kaden says, straight-faced. I can't tell whether he's joking or not and my stomach clenches just thinking about it.

He doesn't make me wait long. Leaning in, his lips feathering over mine, he whispers, "You have a special circle just for you."

His words stop my heart for a moment before I crash my lips to his, tackling him to the bed. The kiss is all tongue and teeth, ravenous like I need to consume him, have him inside me in every sense.

I'm overwhelmed by the magnitude of what I feel for him. I withdraw from the embrace to look him in the eyes, then I form the words I wasn't sure I would ever have the resolve to say. "I want to feel you inside me."

Kaden's eyes widen. "Are you sure? We don't have to."

"I've never been so sure of anything in my entire life."

He kisses me again, this time much softer. We slowly shift positions, Kaden now on top of me. He takes his time removing both our boxers, as if he doesn't want us apart for even a moment. His tongue explores every inch of my mouth while his hands do the same to my body. When his mouth joins his hands, goosebumps erupt all over my skin, sending chills to the tips of my fingers. My entire mind and body are burning with desire, like he's thrown gasoline on a flame inside me that I never knew existed.

He pauses his worship of my skin to reach for the nightstand. Taking out the lube and a condom, he immediately pour the lube on his fingers. I spread my legs, bringing my knees toward my chest like Kaden did the first time I had him under me. I feel the cold gel in my crease as the tips of his fingers circle my hole, and I gasp at his touch. His hand wraps around my hard cock, languidly stroking, both sensations combined making pre-cum leak from my slit.

Kaden begins to apply pressure, and one finger slowly pushes inside me. He must have felt me tense up, because he starts murmuring words of encouragement. "Breathe and try to relax. If you want to stop at any point, just say so." He bends down and kisses my inner thighs. I make eye contact with him and nod.

I take some deep breaths and try to relax all the muscles in my body. Kaden rewards me with a flat tongue licking the groove between my groin and thigh that takes my breath away, followed by a whimper I'm not in the slightest ashamed of making. Kaden nuzzles that same area and begins applying pressure again with his finger, this time pushing past the muscle and slowly pumping into me. It burns a little even with the lube, but soon turns to pleasure as he goes deeper.

Without warning, I feel the warmth of his mouth swallow my dick as far as it can go. At the same time, Kaden crooks his finger, hitting a sweet spot that has me crying out in pleasure, my back arching off the mattress, fingers clutching the sheets.

Kaden rises off my cock with a grin. "I'd like to introduce you to your prostate, Bug."

Just when I think I've caught my breath, he hits it once, twice more. I'm practically sobbing with rapture when he adds another finger, until he's knuckle-deep. He's slowly stroking my cock, and I'm already about to burst from the myriad of sensations shooting through every nerve in my body.

"Kaden please, get inside me now. I can't...I'm going to come if you don't stop." I'm breathless, forcing out every syllable.

"I don't want to hurt you. One more minute—you're doing so good for me, baby," he says as he adds a third finger, scissoring them, stretching me further.

Once again, his approval does things to me. I have to grab the base of my cock and squeeze tightly so I don't come before he's inside me.

His fingers suddenly pull out of me and I could weep at the emptiness. Leaning back, he grabs the condom and rips it open with his teeth. I watch him slide it on and apply generous amounts of lube.

I catch my breath as I feel his head in position, then there's pressure when he slowly slides his way inside me. He leans forward, affectionately placing his soft lips on mine as he pushes and withdraws from me, going in farther an inch at a time with each thrust.

"Breathe. You're taking me so well, baby. Let me in," he whispers against my lips. I can't help but feel that his words mean more than just the physical sense. My vulnerability is at an all-time high, and I'm not even scared. I trust him, wholeheartedly.

When I feel he's about halfway in, I grab his ass and forcefully pull him into me until his trimmed scruff brushes against my balls. Kaden swallows my gasp with a kiss, passionate and heated. His full length inside me feels longer, fuller than I'd imagined. His cock isn't quite as long or thick as mine, but he's still big. If I'm feeling this good with him inside me, I wonder if this is how he feels when our positions are reversed.

Kaden doesn't move a centimeter aside from his mouth's insistent attention on mine. My fingers entangle themselves in his curly locks, pulling him as close as two people can be without becoming one entity.

When we come up for air, Kaden asks, "Are you okay? Did I hurt you?"

I smooth away the worry lines on his forehead with my thumb. "I'm good. Never better, but I need you to start moving." I capture his mouth with mine once again, and slowly, he begins thrusting into me.

I wrap my legs around him, my heels resting on his ass while my hands explore every inch of his skin they can reach. Our soft groans and the sound of our bodies moving together are the only sounds in the room.

"Fuck." He exhales quickly like he was holding his breath, mumbling from where his face is tucked into my neck. "You feel so good, so tight."

Kaden picks up his pace, and the slap sound of skin on skin and filthy cursing joins the erotic harmony of our pleasure.

Above me, he braces himself with a palm next to my head, giving his lower body leverage. His other arm hooks under my knee, raising my leg a little higher, allowing him to go deeper as he pounds relentlessly into me.

Kaden's intense gaze fixed on me does things to me I can't explain. The pressure building in my cock is nearly bursting, and I wrap my fist around myself, making long, fast strokes as tingling sensations shoot from my spine to the tips of my toes

"Kaden, come. Now." I growl out the command seconds before my cum spurts out onto my stomach and chest, and a wordless shout escapes me. Kaden thrusts one last time, deep within me. He buries his face in the crook of my neck as his body jerks and his cock pulses inside me. His long, drawn-out groan is muffled by his lips on my skin.

Kaden's body collapses onto mine, both of us breathless and sweaty, my cum a mess between our bodies.

Kaden's lips caress my neck and earlobe, and I feel his breath in my ear as he whispers, "I love you."

The explosion inside my ribcage I can only assume is my heart combusting from elation.

Three simple words. That's all it took to feel whole.

Chapter Twenty-Three

WE ALL NEED SOMEONE

Kaden

*D*ear *Goddesses, please tell me I didn't say what I think I said.*

Nice job scaring the fuck out of the one guy we actually like, Kaden.

It's too soon. He's going to freak out and leave. I have to explain it was a heat-of-the moment kind of thing. I didn't mean it. He'll understand.

"Uh, sorry. That's not what I meant to say. I got carried away in the moment." I laugh nervously as I give the worst excuse ever. I haven't moved my head from where I dropped it on his shoulder. I can't look him in the eye right now. He'll see through my lies.

"I love you, Kaden."

Lifting my head slowly, I see a tear falling down his cheek. "I didn't say it to make you feel like you should too. You don't have to feel obligated," I whisper, afraid I'll break down from all the emotions flowing through me right now.

"I love you, Kaden."

"You said that already." A smile forms on my face at how cute he is right now. "Why are you crying, Luke?"

He looks confused. "I didn't realize I was." He goes to wipe the tear away. I stop his hand and sweep my tongue across his cheek instead, taking his tears. They're mine now.

He cups my face with both hands, pulling me in, and placing a delicate kiss on my lips. "I love you, Kaden."

"I love you, Luke." I don't know what's going on here, but it seems like something more. He's staring at me like he's seen a ghost.

I pull out of him and move to his side, removing the condom to throw it in the bedside trash bin. Luke is staring up at the ceiling now. I stand, offering my hand, and he takes it.

I guide him to the bathroom. Closing the toilet lid, I have him sit while I run a hot bath. He's staring down at his hands in his lap now. Is he in shock? Does he regret this?

I kneel down in front of him while we wait for the tub to fill. "Luke, are you okay? You're kind of scaring me."

His gaze meets mine. With a softness in his smile, he says, "Yeah, Kaden. I'm perfect."

I swear, his smile can melt an iceberg. "C'mon, Bug. Let's get you in the bath. I'm sure you're sore."

He stands, and I help him into the garden-style tub, following as he leans forward for me to slide in behind him. I wrap my legs around his front where he rests his arms on them and leans back against my chest.

"Want to talk about it?" I ask him cautiously, not wanting to poke my nose where it shouldn't be.

He's quiet for a minute, then another. I wait him out. I won't push him to tell me something he's not ready to talk about. I massage his arms and shoulders, hoping to relax him if nothing else.

"I've never had anyone say, 'I love you' to me before."

Oh.

"You've never been in love?"

"No. But I mean like ever, from anyone besides my aunts and Gabe. But somehow that doesn't count. I never doubted their love."

"I don't quite understand, Luke."

He hesitates. "My family isn't full of the most affectionate people. We never said, 'I love you.' My mother hugged us every once in a while, but besides that, any display of love was nonexistent."

It takes me a minute to process what he said. "What about Jackson or Dakota? I'm sure they've told you they love you, right?"

"They grew up in the same family. I know they love me, I suppose. We never say it, though. We don't really talk about emotions or anything remotely close to it."

"What about your dad? The same with him?"

"Yeah. I think my father's parents are where it started, at least for my immediate family. My grandparents were that way with my father and Uncle Jack, Dakota's dad. Once they had kids, it just became a thing. They both treated us all like we were soldiers, born to follow the path set for us going back generations. Police officers in every one of them. Small-town families full of police officers are a different breed. I think my mother and Aunt Jean, Dakota's mother, started out differently, both showing the three of us at least some affection. About the time I was seven years old, my father started telling them to stop babying us. Jack agreed, and reinforced it with, 'They'll never make it on the force acting like a bunch of crybabies.' God forbid a five-year-old cry because he fell out of his treehouse and broke his wrist."

Luke drops his head back onto my shoulder, inhaling deeply and letting it out in a big whoosh. "After that, I started spending every moment I could with my aunts. I would beg my mom to let me go spend weekends with them, or on school breaks. I spent summers mostly with them. I think my mom knew why, too. I've had more happy memories with them than anyone else in my family. They're a lot of fun, and I never doubted their love for me. They made sure I knew it too."

"They sound like good people." I smile and kiss his cheek.

"The best. I don't know where I'd be without them."

"Have you ever spoken to your parents about it? Told them how you felt as a kid and still do?"

"Every time I'd come home from spending time with my aunts, I was in the habit of saying, 'I love you' with them. I slipped and said it to my father a couple times." He pauses, his hands tightening around my ankles where they were resting. "He would ignore me and walk away like he didn't hear me. I didn't dare mention it to my parents. It would just make it hurt more."

I snake my arms around his chest, squeezing tightly. "I'm sorry they made you feel unloved."

He takes my hand in his, raising it to his lips, kissing my palm. "I'm sorry I killed the mood."

"You didn't do anything wrong. I'm glad you shared this with me."

"Trauma dumping right after you said, 'I love you' for the first time probably wasn't what you were expecting from me." Luke chuckles, shaking his head at himself.

"I guess I'll have to keep telling you how much I love you until the trauma is a long-gone memory. I love you, Luke," I say, kissing his temple. "I love you, Luke." His cheek. "I love you, Luke." His shoulder. "Almost gone, or should I keep going?"

Luke twists his body, facing me to the best of his ability in the small space, making water slosh around and onto the floor. "Never stop." His mouth takes complete control of mine. The fervor behind it, physically and emotionally, feels like molten lava burning beneath my skin, taking my soul with it to bring it home. To him.

He's in love with me.

One Week Later

Please, make them stop.

"Ladies, please. You're giving me a headache already, and we haven't even gotten to the diner yet," I plead with Faith and Lanie to stop bickering. They hardly ever get on each other's nerves, but Lanie leaving her clothes in the dryer overnight has Faith's panties in a bunch for some odd reason.

"I'm sorry, but I don't understand why you're so annoyed by it. I got them out first thing this morning, didn't I?"

Lanie's weird way of apologizing does the trick, or maybe Faith is finally done with her mood swing. "Fine. I'm sorry too."

"Do you still love me?" Lanie jokes.

"That's a dumb question. Always." I catch Faith rolling her eyes in my rearview mirror. I know the ice breaks a little more when I see the corner of her mouth rise as Lanie reaches from the passenger seat to grab her hand.

I pull into the diner's lot, parking next to Ender's car where he and Connor are waiting for us. I can hear them bickering through the closed windows.

We're surrounded by a bunch of children.

"I'm starving. Hurry, let's go." Ender says as he gets out of the car. He seems to be in a good mood today—actually smiling—well, sort of. At least for him. At any rate, it's more of a smile than a frown.

We get seated and order right away. Connor and Lanie fill the room with chatter right away, as usual. Faith is on her phone looking annoyed, reading text messages. Ender is on his phone, too, but at least he seems content. Is that a real smile on his face now?

"Guys, I want to make a reservation at Stonewood's for a Saturday a week or two after they open. Who wants to go with me?" All their attention shifts when four sets of eyes look my way.

"I've already promised Jackson and Dakota I'd go with them and their aunts the weekend after they open. Can I take a rain check?" Lanie gives an apologetic smile.

I haven't been introduced to the aunts yet, so I understand why I wasn't invited with them. It didn't escape me that Faith perked up from her phone for a split second when Lanie mentioned who she was going with, though.

"Faith do you want to come with me?"

"Yeah, sounds like fun." She puts her phone down, seeming more present

"You know I'm coming whether you like it or not," Connor shares, unprompted.

"That goes without saying." I agree with him. "Ender, what about you?"

"You don't think we'd be distracting them?"

I noticed he used 'them,' not Luke. "I think *they* would like to see us both there." Luke accidentally let it slip the other day that Gabe has been texting back and forth with Ender lately. I haven't mentioned it because neither has Ender. He will when he's ready.

Ender nods his head, "Okay, sounds good. Count me in." He seems pleased with his decision, and it makes my heart happy for him. He deserves someone special.

Our food comes with perfect timing, just as he starts complaining again about his stomach growling, and the meal is filled with laughter with the closest people in my life, sans Luke.

Since our confessions, we've been spending a lot of time together. I've slept over at his place almost the entire week. He gave me an extra key by mid-week, figuring it was better than waiting at home or in my car until he got home. I've fallen asleep in his bed with Fred every night since. He and I have become best buddies. I've noticed the nights I'm half asleep, Luke doesn't even attempt to wake me up any longer, instead sliding in next to me and pulling me to him for snuggles. I have to admit he really is the best snuggler. Inevitably, we wake up not being able to keep our hands off each other, and I'm not complaining at all. Being inside Luke is my new favorite thing.

His family dynamic was a little shocking at first, given how well-adjusted all three of them seem. I don't know how I would've turned out if my parents weren't as affectionate as they are to us. I see how Ender is most of the time. That kind of trauma, albeit emotional, not physical, thank Goddesses, still affects so much of you. It can change who you are as a person. I'm so glad that behavior didn't sink its teeth into Luke.

Remind me to thank his aunts.

Chapter Twenty-Four Part One

Your Reaction to the Events of Life Means More Than the Event Itself

Luke

The first two weeks after opening have gone somewhat smoothly considering most restaurants struggle in the beginning. There were a couple of hiccups, but Gabe and I, along with the staff, rectified the issues quickly enough for them to not affect the guests' experiences.

I'm currently stuck behind the bar, cleaning up some broken glass. We're almost at full capacity, and one of the bartenders, obviously very busy, didn't notice the other standing behind him. During the collision, he dropped the glass he was holding, shattering it to pieces. I could get some help from the bussers, but I am more of a hands-on type of guy. I want my staff to know we are here for them.

I catch a glimpse of Faith's fiery red hair and know immediately my boyfriend is nearby. I chuckle at myself, thinking I'd never be saying those words before meeting Kaden, my boyfriend. Now, they instantly put a smile on my face. I quickly finish my task and head their way.

"This is unexpected," I say as I approach the large circular booth they're seated in. Kaden turns my way, smiling from ear to ear.

"We wanted to surprise you. Hope we aren't taking you away from something important." Typical Kaden, always worried about inconveniencing others.

I lean down into him. "Nothing is more important than you." Then I place a kiss on his blushing cheek.

"Well, well, well, who do we have here?" Gabe, of course, joins us. I know it's because he noticed Ender sitting with Kaden, Connor, and Faith. He's trying to play it cool, but he's been the one smiling at his phone more often than not lately.

"Hey, Gabe. Congratulations on opening. It looks great in here. Full house." Kaden greets him first.

"Yeah, congratulations, guys. You've done an amazing job here." Ender doesn't hesitate to join in, although his eyes are glued to Gabe's the whole time.

"Thanks. It means a lot." Gabe catches himself gawking at Ender and redirects his attention to the rest of the group. "Glad you could all join us."

"We have to get back to work. There's plenty of stuff to do around here tonight." I pat Gabe on the back. "Enjoy your dinner and order whatever you want—it's on us. I'll be back around later." I direct the latter part towards Kaden, followed by mouthing the words, "I love you." He returns the sentiment.

I'll never get sick of it.

"Oh, one more thing." I get close enough for Kaden to feel my breath on his cheek. "You look really good tonight, and if I wouldn't be jealous of anyone else getting to hear the way you moan and beg for more when I finally get to suck your cock, I'd be ripping your clothes off and dropping

138

to my knees for you right now." I realize I said that a little louder than I probably should have when Kaden starts feigning a tickle in his throat as a distraction. I didn't think anyone heard me until I glance at the group, hearing snickering coming from Faith and Connor. I wink at Kaden, knowing I'll be in trouble for that later. I can't wait.

Walking away, I tease Gabe, "What was that you said to me a month or so ago? Oh yeah, you've got it bad, my friend." I laugh at him shoving me with his elbow.

"Shut up, dickhead," he mumbles under his breath. "Go back to picking on your boyfriend instead of me."

Everything has been going smoothly since the broken glass incident, thankfully. I'm standing near the bar, talking with Gabe and a guest having dinner there by himself, when I look over to see how Kaden and our friends are doing. They look like they're almost done with their meals.

I attempt to tune back into the conversation with Gabe and the guest, but I see Kaden's eyes widen, his skin turning white as a ghost. I follow his line of sight to a couple walking past their table. The guy with his hand on the small of the woman's back does a double take at him and smirks, and Kaden quickly drops his chin to his chest, avoiding any further eye contact.

What the fuck was that? Rather, who the fuck is that?

The hairs on the back of my neck are standing on end just from witnessing the brief interaction. I politely wrap up the conversation with the guest and turn back toward Kaden to see that he's gone. My eyes dart to the table where the couple was seated not far from him, finding the woman by herself, reading the menu.

I move with purpose toward the restroom hallway, guessing it's the only place Kaden would have gone with the rest of our friends still at their table. When I get there, I see Kaden up against the wall, facing the floor. The guy is standing in front of him, too closely for an ordinary conversation.

I can't hear what he's saying as I approach them, but he's whispering something to Kaden.

"Kaden, is there a problem here?" Kaden's head pops up, his eyes meeting mine with desperation.

The guy—Tyler, if my assumption is correct—answers for him, "No problem here, just talking to an old friend."

"Old friends talk with each other, not at each other. And Kaden doesn't look like he feels like talking with you. So, let me introduce myself. I'm Luke, Kaden's boyfriend. Who are you?"

"Tyler, old dental school buddy of Kaden's." Tyler extends his hand.

If my eyes had the fire I feel in my veins shooting out of them, they would sear his hand right off during the brief moment it takes me to decide he isn't worthy of any further attention.

I keep my wits about the situation, knowing I can't cause a scene in my own restaurant. Instead of responding to Tyler, I look at Kaden. "Can I please walk you back to your table?"

Kaden nods, taking my hand when I wrap the other around his waist and begin walking down the hallway with him. We get only a few steps away before Tyler says, "It was nice seeing you, Kaden. Keep in touch."

Kaden doesn't move, but I do. I find myself standing nearly toe-to-toe with Tyler, my tone dripping with loathing. "I know who you are and what you did. I will say this one time. Stay the fuck away from Kaden. Don't come near him ever again, or you and I are going to have a problem." I don't wait for a response. I meet Kaden where I left him, and continue walking with him as far away from Tyler as possible. At the end of the hallway, Gabe's furrowed brows and pursed lips tell me he witnessed enough to understand something isn't right here.

"Do I need to escort him out of the building?" Gabe asks, the fury in his eyes aimed behind us.

"No. Leave him be. We can't risk him causing any more of a scene. Can you go get the rest and tell them to meet us outside, please?"

"Will do. Kaden, are you okay?" Gabe, being the good man he is, checks on his new friend.

Kaden nods, a glazed-over look in his eyes.

I escort Kaden out the front doors and step to the side, avoiding obstructing the pathway. My hands cup his face. "Kaden, are you okay? Did he touch you?"

"Yeah, I'm fine. Thank you for coming for me. I didn't..." He pauses, clearly thinking. "I'm sorry I took you away from your work."

The group comes rushing out of the restaurant in a panic, Ender in the lead. "Kaden, what happened?"

"I'm fine. I promise. Everybody, stop worrying." Kaden's attempt to reassure us falls flat.

"Guys, can I have a second with Kaden, please?" I look at our friends one-by-one, ending my gaze on Ender.

Ender looks from me to his friend for approval. "I'm good." Kaden assures him.

Once alone, I address his worry of taking me away from work, "You need to understand something. You come first. The restaurant and the guests, Gabe can handle. If you need me, ever, for anything, you are my priority. Don't ever think any differently. Do you understand?" Kaden stares in disbelief. "Kaden, tell me you understand, please."

"Yes." He looks down at his feet.

I pinch his chin and bring his face upright. "I love you."

"I love you." He tenderly responds.

I take his hand and walk back to the group. Gabe has joined us outside now.

"Who drove Kaden here?" I address the group.

Ender raises a finger in the air.

"Can I trust you to take him home, walk him to his apartment door, and not leave until he is inside, and the door is locked?"

Ender looks shocked. "That's not even a question, but out of respect, yes, absolutely."

"That's a bit extreme, isn't it? There's no need to do that." Kaden, being Kaden, doesn't want to be an inconvenience. I hate whoever convinced him he was. I can probably guess that's a side effect of that asshole sitting inside.

I refuse to ever let him think that way about himself when it comes to me. "He hurt you once. I won't let it happen again. I protect what's mine, Angel."

"Swoon," Faith and Connor say together in matching cutesy voices.

I give them a 'really guys?' type of look, to which they both reply, "What?"

It's scary how similar they are if you look deep enough. They just express themselves differently most of the time.

Returning my attention back to Kaden, I wrap my arms around him and kiss his forehead. "I'll be over once I finish up here. I'll text you when I'm in your building. Don't open it until you hear my voice."

"Okay." Kaden shakes his head at me but gives me a smile anyway.

"See you soon."

Chapter Twenty-Four Part Two

I Know Who Truly Cares For Me

Kaden

F aith and Connor are chattering on and on in the back seat about Tyler being a psycho for following me into the restroom, and how hot Luke is for protecting me. I have to agree—it was pretty hot when he threatened Tyler.

When I spotted Tyler and his wife coming our way, I froze. Making eye contact sent me into panic mode. The bastard fucking smirked at me. I've never hated anyone in my life like I hated him in that moment. I went to the restroom to splash some water on my face, knowing if I stayed where I was, I may have made a scene. I couldn't do that to Luke.

When I came out of the restroom, Tyler was there.

"It's good to see you, Kaden."

"Leave me alone, Tyler. Go have dinner with your wife and forget I was here."

"What's wrong? I thought you'd be happy to see me." Tyler steps in closer.

"What could possibly make you think that?"

"I don't know. Maybe because we were together for a long time. I thought we loved each other. I know I loved you." He raises his hand to my face, imitating a gentle touch.

"Tyler, do not touch me." I slap his hand away, and Tyler gets right in my face.

"Don't. I'm trying to be nice." His tone turns from seething to tender so fast it gives me whiplash. "I've missed you. Haven't you missed me?" His face is an inch from mine, and I duck my head to avoid eye contact with him.

"Kaden, is there a problem here?"

I'll never forget the moment Luke walked into that hallway.

"Kaden, you okay?" Ender knows I'm in my head.

"Yeah, I'm good. It wasn't something I was prepared for, but I'll be fine."

"What did he say to you?" Faith asks from the back.

"Nothing worth a damn. More lies, that's all."

"God, I wish Luke would have decked him. I would have given anything to see that." Connor loves drama more than anyone I know. His obsession with reality TV shows is out of control.

We arrive at my house before anyone else can add their two cents. Faith and Connor get out to hug me—they know I need it right now. Ender leaves the car running, following me into my building.

"Luke is umm... Something else," Ender says when the elevator doors close. "You guys are getting pretty serious, huh?"

"I'd say so," I tell him, smiling at the thought.

"I'm glad. He's a good guy."

"Yeah, he is."

The doors open, and Ender throws his arm around my shoulders, pulling me into his side as we walk to my apartment door.

"You know I love you, right?" Ender says.

"Of course, always." I kiss his head when he turns and hugs me, then nudges me toward the door.

"Now get in there, or Luke will come kick my ass."

"Thanks. I'll call you tomorrow," I laugh at him feigning fear.

I lock the door behind me and walk straight to the couch. I'm so mentally exhausted from the evening's events that all I want to do is lie down. Pulling the blanket off the back of the couch, I curl up with it and drift to sleep.

Chapter Twenty-Five

PROTECTING WHAT'S MINE
HAS ITS BENEFITS

Luke

"**Y**ou going to be okay, buddy?" Gabe asks for the tenth time since Kaden left tonight.

"I'm okay. I want to get home to Kaden. You good if I get going?" The doors have been locked for about a half hour now.

"Go. Take tomorrow off. I'll handle it here." I hug my best friend before rushing out the door.

When Kaden left the restaurant earlier, I didn't take my eyes off Tyler for the rest of the night. The fucker actually had the audacity to grin at me as he walked out the door later. Had Gabe not been standing next to me at that moment, grabbing my shoulder, I would've walked out to the parking lot behind him.

I wonder what his wife would think of the shit he pulled tonight. I don't know what he said to Kaden, yet, but I can guarantee his wife wouldn't like it and probably doesn't even know about Kaden at all.

I park outside Kaden's building and take my phone out, dialing his number when I enter the foyer. He doesn't answer on the first try. I try again, entering the elevator. It doesn't connect, the elevator blocking my signal. Walking faster down his hallway than usual, I dial his number again. Reaching Kaden's door, I try the handle and knock hard when it doesn't move.

"Hey I'm here. I'm coming." Kaden's sleepy voice finally answers the call. It disconnects as the lock disengages, then he opens the door, still rubbing his eyes. Without saying anything, I crash into him, relieved to have him back in my arms.

"Luke, I need to breathe." Kaden's muffled voice against my chest makes me smile. I loosen my grip on him and lock the door behind me. "I'm sorry I didn't answer right away. I fell asleep on the couch."

"It's okay, I just got worried. Did you sleep long?" He looks at the clock on the microwave. It's after 11 p.m. now, so he's been home for about three hours.

"I passed out just after I got home." He wraps his arms around my neck, pulling me closer, hitting me with those sultry eyes, his lips rendering me breathless.

Releasing me, he takes my hand and walks me to his bedroom. When the door closes behind us, the air in the room changes. The heat in Kaden's eyes is immeasurable.

He's standing so close I can feel his breath on my lips when he says, "Do you know how sexy you were defending me? Threatening someone in my honor?"

The way Kaden unabashedly undresses me with his eyes as they roam down my body and back up to my face again sends blood rushing straight to my cock. "You like when I let someone know you're mine? Does that turn you on, Kaden?" It's my turn to undress him, but not figuratively. I grab the hem of his shirt only to have my hand forcefully knocked away.

"It does, in ways you couldn't imagine." He leans in, warm breath kissing the nerve endings in my earlobes, making the hairs on the back of my neck stand up. The commanding allure exuding through his words stuns me. "On your knees, Luke. Now."

This man continues to amaze me more every single day. I drop to my knees without a second thought, knowing I would do anything he asked of me.

Choosing his words purposefully, Kaden smirks, "Good boy."

I inhale deeply, my eyes close of their own volition and roll backwards.

He fists my hair, pulling my head backward so that I'm looking up, his authoritative presence demanding attention. "Did I say you can close your eyes?"

"No." Reading the room, I add, "Sir." Kaden's nostrils flare. Letting go of my hair, he stands upright, his hard cock at eye level. He notices my attention on his arousal, and I wait for further instructions, knowing how much better it's all going to feel if I just let go.

"Take it out." I quickly oblige, loving every second of Kaden taking control. He was right when he said he loved when I took control—it's incomparably erotic.

His cock stands fully erect, inches from my mouth. I haven't had the privilege to suck him off yet, not that I haven't wanted to try, but we're always too eager to be inside each other. I want this more than anything right now; the need to swallow his cock takes every fiber of my being to resist until I'm given further instructions.

"Stick your tongue in my slit."

When the tip of my tongue pushes into him, his body shivers. It delights me that I did that to him.

"Put my cock in your mouth until it hits the back of your throat."

I take a deep breath and do as I'm told. When the head approaches my throat, though, I gag and withdraw.

"Try again. Breathe through your nose. Don't think about it so much."

I do as he says, relaxing my throat and breathing through my nose. This time, I get him back farther without feeling the gagging sensation as much.

"Swallow."

Kaden's control falters for a brief moment as I swallow around him. A loud, gravelly groan forms in his throat, faintly vibrating my eardrums.

He tangles his fingers in my hair and begins pumping into me slowly, giving me time to acclimate to the rhythm. I suck on him with every withdrawal, watching as his head lolls back, mouth agape. The physical feeling of having Kaden in my mouth fills me with pure lust, but his facial expressions and the carnal noises coming from us while I'm sucking his cock are downright pornographic.

My hands instinctively grab the back of his thighs. He stops abruptly, pulling completely out of my mouth. I take the moment to catch my breath.

"Did I say you could put your hands on me?"

"No, sir."

He glances sternly at me, albeit clearly enjoying himself. "Strip. Get on the bed. Face to the mattress, ass in the air. Now." My heart is pounding with the anticipation of what's to come. I've loved every second of Kaden being inside me since first experiencing it. Right now, it's turned into a need. I rush to obey him. As soon as I do, Kaden undresses fully and moves to the nightstand, grabbing his supplies and throwing them on the bed.

Once in position, and without any warning, the room echoes with a loud slap. A stinging sensation on each of my ass cheeks follows, and I jerk forward. Sealing my lips tightly, I muffle my groan, taking my punishment with pleasure.

Soft palms caress my burning flesh. "Does my Bug like being under my control?"

"More than you can possibly imagine." I breathe out each word with passion.

He huffs at me. "Maybe next time you'll think twice about teasing me in public with promises you can't keep." His palms on my ass spread me wide. I sense how close he is when I feel the warmth of his breath ghost across my skin. The moment his tongue skims across my hole, I'm whimpering, internally begging for more. I want it all, everything he has to give me.

He licks a long stroke from my balls up my crease, circles his tongue around my hole and pushes in with the tip. The act is now in my top five favorite things Kaden has done to me. His tongue pumping in and out of me has my cock about to beg Kaden to let me show it the attention it desperately needs right now. My fists clench around the pillow above my head, fighting to control the urge.

I see Kaden in my periphery, reaching for the lube, then his tongue is gone. It's replaced by his cold, gelled fingers massaging my hole, lasting only seconds before his index finger is shoved fully inside me in one quick motion. I gasp from the sudden intrusion. He doesn't move any further, allowing me a moment to adjust.

"If it gets too much, tell me. Full stop. No questions asked."

I nod vehemently, giving him full permission to use my body as he sees fit.

He hooks his finger downward towards my belly and brushes my prostate, sending shooting sensations into the base of my spine. Pumping in and out of me at a slow pace, a second finger then joining while his free hand reaches around to fist my cock, it's thankful for his touch. The noises leaving my body are foreign to me. The ecstasy coursing through me heightens when he shoves a third finger into me, and his pace quickens. The hand on my cock hasn't moved aside from tightening and releasing while thumbing over the tip. I need him to stroke it so badly, but I know I'm at his mercy. He's teasing my cock while stretching me. The combination is offensive—an attack on my willpower with no remorse—but I'll take it willingly, for him.

"Do you like me using your body, Luke?" he whispers. "The pain turning into pleasure? Me abusing your hole like it's my playground? Tell me what you want. What do you need?"

"More," is the only word I can seem to form.

When he crooks all three fingers, pressing harder than the last time, I collapse on the bed with a moaning cry that echoes throughout the room. His attack on my hole halts as he withdraws his fingers and goes to grab the condom off the bed.

I grab his wrist, stopping him. With my face still resting on the mattress, I breathlessly tell him, "Bare. I tested negative a couple weeks ago. Please."

"I tested negative over a month ago, and I'm on PrEP. Are you sure?"

"Without any doubt. I trust you." I let go of his wrist when he leans down, kissing me softly.

His demeanor changes. "Can you get up?" I nod, turning over to sit up.

He slides back on the bed, positioning his back against the headboard. "Ride me."

The love coursing through me right now is unfathomable. He's changed his original plans, giving me control instead.

Straddling him, I kiss him hungrily. Then I reach for his cock and align him, slowly sinking down until my balls are pressed against his pelvis. With nothing between us, I can feel the heat of him inside me, every sensation more intense.

I brace my hands on his shoulders as I lean back and start undulating on his cock. His hands squeeze my hips, our eyes locked in a powerful embrace. Earning the love of this man will forever be my greatest accomplishment. I'm overwhelmed with emotions, and tears well in my eyes as I continue riding him.

Kaden leans in, cupping my face, and gently kisses me. He licks my tears away, one cheek at a time, then returns his lips to mine. Barely whispering, he tells me, "Take what you need from me." He leans back and bends his knees, encouraging me by thrusting upward at the moment I fall onto his cock. I place my hand on his shoulder, the other behind me on his thigh, and begin spearing myself on him, quickening my pace.

Both of us are sweaty messes, our panting and groaning like music to my ears. "Fuck, you're killing me. You feel so good. Don't stop, please." Kaden's pleading sets me on fire.

"I'm going to come," Kaden warns, attempting to lift me off him. I brush his hands away and fist my cock, aggressively stroking, wanting to come with him. *Needing* to come with him.

I feel him begin to pulse inside me, the warmth of his cum squirting into me, and his moaning sends me over the edge. Pulling off his cock, I aim mine at his face, erupting all over him with a shout of ecstasy. The soul-deep gratification on his face matches my own as I mark him.

Catching my breath, I lean forward to lick his lips, sweeping up my release and sharing it with him in a sinful kiss. My cum, now his.

I feel his fingers caress my hole, his cum seeping out of me. He wipes it up and pushes it back inside me, marking me from the inside.

I've never felt more connected to anyone in my entire life.

I wake up wrapped in Kaden's arms feeling like I'm attached to a radiator. How could anyone be naked and still give off this much heat? I peel my sticky body from his, knowing I need another shower now. After the mess we made of each other last night, we took a bath together again. I've never even liked baths before meeting Kaden. Hell, there are a lot of things I thought I didn't like before meeting him. Honestly, I find it hard to resist anything when it comes to him.

"Where are you going?" Kaden's groggy morning voice whines from behind me. I don't get a chance to respond before his arms wrap around me, pulling me back onto the bed.

I laugh at his resistance to getting out of bed, coming from the man who is used to getting up by six in the morning to run. "C'mon out of bed. We're going out today."

"Do we have to?" Kaden hangs his leg over my hip, hooking it around me in an attempt to keep me in place.

"Yes, we have to. Don't tempt me to stay in bed. I have the day off, and I'm taking you somewhere. Up, now, mister."

He releases me, only to whine more when I make my way to the bathroom to shower. Lucky for me, he follows and gives me that beautiful view of him looking up at me through his long lashes and swallows my cum as if it's his favorite meal of the day.

He pushes my hand away when I attempt to touch him. "Later." I can see the sinful thoughts all over his face.

We finish getting ready in record time and head out to feed Fred first. Pulling Kaden away from Fred-cuddles gets harder every time they're together. I think he loves Kaden more than he loves me, now.

Traitor. Maybe people are right—cats have no loyalty. I'll just have to win him back with more treats.

"First on the agenda: breakfast." Kaden's grumpy side is going to come out if I don't get food and coffee in his belly soon.

"I know the perfect spot." I'm hesitant about not warning him where we are going, but I know how anxious he gets about meeting new people. Hopefully not telling him doesn't backfire.

We walk in to the aroma of baked blueberries permeating the café.

"Luke!" The gleeful voice overpowers the cacophony of espresso machines, chatter of multiple conversations, and ambient music.

"Good morning, G." Grace's hugs are comparable to Lanie's, and their similar stature makes for backaches for me.

"Well, who do we have here? Hello, cutie pie. You keeping my Luke here in line? If he gives you any trouble, you come talk to me, you hear?" The warmth in Kaden's expression while Grace gives him a matching backache is evidence that I'm not actually in trouble.

"Nice to meet you...G?" Kaden looks to me for validation.

"Grace," I clarify for him, but G slaps my stomach.

"You hush now. He can call me 'G' if he wants to. Anybody who can tie you down for more than a night is basically family at this point."

Kaden's shoulders shake with amusement, and my cheeks heat.

"Now, now, Grace. Quit bothering the boy. We don't want to scare off the first man Luke has had the balls to bring home to meet us." Aunt Brenda throws her arm around her wife's waist, giving us some breathing room.

"Wait, have there been other men, Luke? You told her, but not me? What the hell? I thought I was your favorite!"

I love Brenda more than I can put into words, but G knows I favor her and likes to point it out whenever possible to tease her wife, even though I'd never say it aloud. Brenda is my role model in every way. She shaped me into the man I am today, and I couldn't be more grateful. G was the one who suffocated me with love and affection, knowing at times I needed it more than anything else.

"No, G. Kaden is my first boyfriend."

The approval on her face embarrasses me a little more, and she's proud of it.

"Would you boys like some coffee and breakfast? C'mon, a batch of those blueberry muffins you love came out of the oven a few minutes ago, Luke." Brenda hooks her arm through Kaden's, leading us to the back of the café where they have their own little space cornered off. "So, Kaden, tell us all about yourself. Pretend like Luke hasn't been gushing about you for the past month."

"I thought we weren't trying to scare him off, Brenda?"

"Nonsense. I was only giving Grace shit for not telling me you were here. If this guy scares off that easily, he isn't built to be in this family."

"I can see where Luke gets his boldness and incredible sense of humor from." Kaden's laughter nearly bursts my heart into pieces.

For the next hour, I watch my three favorite people in this world enjoy each other's company—mostly laughing at my expense—but I'll take it any day if this is the outcome. G may or may not have attempted to bribe Kaden into marrying me, claiming, "He needs someone who looks at him the way you do." I swear, that woman is a wild card. When we all agree it's time to get on with the day, I have to pry Kaden from my aunts' arms, promising we'll visit again soon.

"So, that wasn't too bad of a surprise?" I feel Kaden shaking with laughter from where my hand is on his lower back. I'm glad he's amused.

"No, you're not in trouble, Luke. It was a nice surprise. They're a lot of fun to be around."

"Good, because now that they've met you, they're going to want to see you all the time. I can guarantee one of them will be texting me for your phone number by bedtime tonight." Given the huge grin on his face, I'm guessing he won't mind that at all.

During the short drive to Freedom Park, Kaden chatters on about how nice my aunts are, and how he can't wait to introduce them to his mom.

He insists they'll get along like three peas in a pod. I have no doubt that, knowing Kaden and Lanie, their mother is amazing, as well.

"Okay, now that you threw me into meeting 'the parents'"—he literally uses air quotes on me—"you're joining Sunday dinner and game night."

"Wait, tonight?"

"Hey, at least I'm warning you beforehand." Kaden's fingers tapping away on his phone, let me know I am in this whether I like it or not. "Mom said she can't wait to meet you, and you'd better bring your A-game for some shit-talking with my dad."

I wipe my brow, feeling the temperature in the car rise a few degrees almost instantaneously. Kaden's faint laughter is barely noticeable through the anxiety pulsing in my ears.

"Luke, you have nothing to worry about, I promise. They'll love you." Kaden's attempts to reassure me don't do the trick.

"I've never met anyone's parents. I'm fucking thirty years old. Why does this scare the hell out of me like I'm a sixteen-year-old boy?"

Because I love him. If his parents don't like me, then what?

Kaden's hands wrap around my face as I put the Jeep in park, pulling my lips to meet his. His touch has my shoulders lowering, my thoughts no longer racing out of control. I'll never understand how he has this much power to ease my mind.

Chapter Twenty-Six

IT WAS ALMOST A PERFECT DAY

Kaden

Luke being worried about meeting my parents is adorable, but unnecessary. "Bug, relax. Let's have a nice afternoon. You'll see, there's no reason to worry."

"Alright. I'm fine." He looks a little calmer now as we get out and begin our walk through the park.

The sun shining brightly and the warm, soft breeze—despite it being the end of March—make for the perfect day. Walking around the lake, the park is busy with people doing all sorts of activities, excited to be out and about after being cooped up all winter. We pass a group doing yoga on a large grassy area, and some families out enjoying a nice walk.

We walk in a comfortable silence, Luke holding my hand the whole time. I love that he's never shied away from showing me affection in public. Quite a difference from Tyler, that's for sure. I can't believe I ever compared Luke to him.

"You said you wanted to know everything about me," I start. "Weird fact number one: I love to people-watch." I don't know why, but I'm not nervous about sharing this with him.

"Why is that weird? People-watching is great. You learn far more about people that way than anything else."

"I guess it's weird because I hate being in crowded areas, but they make for the best people-watching."

"Brenda and G once told me they would go to amusement parks when they first met, and just people-watch all day. Half the time, they didn't even bother going on rides. You should hear some of their stories."

I lead us toward the stone bridge over one end of the lake, where there's a pretty spot to take pictures. At the foot of the bridge, a man is walking around, handing out roses. He gives me a white rose when we walk past him.

"Thank you. That's sweet," I say to him.

"You gentlemen have a nice day." The older man offers the kindest smile, then moves on to another couple.

At the top of the bridge, we stop and lean over the edge of the wall. Luke now holds my free hand with both of his, rubbing his thumbs across my knuckles, his smile aimed right at me. "Your smile is as bright as the sun right now. You like roses that much?" My reaction to the rose seems to intrigue him.

"Growing up, my father would buy my mother a bouquet of roses once a month, without fail. Every time, there were twelve red roses, and one white."

"Was there a significance of the one white rose?" Luke's genuine interest in everything we talk about fills me with warm, fuzzy feelings. Nothing is more attractive than a man who is truly engaged in your conversations.

"When I was about eleven years old, I asked my father the same question. He said the white rose represents love and loyalty. My parents met in middle school and became instant friends. Well, you can see what that led to." I motion to myself. "They've been married for almost thirty years. He still buys her those thirteen roses every month. I don't think he's ever missed a month all these years." I feel my cheeks starting to hurt, thinking about how special their love story is.

"That's really nice. I'm glad you had such a strong example of love growing up."

His wistful tone has my anxiety mounting. "Luke, I'm sorry. I didn't mean to bring up a sore subject."

He squeezes my hand, forcing me to look his way with a tug. "Don't ever apologize for sharing a happy memory. My weird family dynamic is not your fault. You don't have to walk on eggshells because of it."

With a nod, I take my phone out and lean in close to him. I don't want to linger on the subject and make him uncomfortable. We hold numerous poses while I snap away. I even licked his cheek in one of them, telling him he's now mine. He didn't bother to argue. My favorite is of us sharing a kiss, sun rays shining above us, and the smiles on our faces gleaming with love. I would gladly spend the rest of my life showing him the love he deserves if he'd let me.

Whoa.

We arrive at my parents' house a little after 4 p.m., just in time to help my parents with dinner. My mother, excited that I'm finally bringing Luke to meet them, had said he'd better be ready for some of her basic cooking. She downplays her dishes, even though they're always delicious. When we walk into the house, I smell garlic cooking right away. It's truly my favorite aroma in the world. Mom puts garlic in everything, and the smell of it cooking always feels like home to me.

The creak of the floor in the hallway leading to the kitchen alerts my parents, who quickly come around the corner. If someone asked me to describe my mother's expression, pure exhilaration would be an understatement. I think she may scare Luke off before we even get a chance to eat.

"Hello parental units. I beg you, please don't embarrass me." My parents, being two of the most unserious people in this type of situation, both react as expected.

"Who, us? Honey, did he call us weird? Should I be offended?" My father always looking to my mother for guidance is one of the funniest things to me.

"You know, dear, I think you're right. We should probably be offend-ed. Kaden, whatever do you mean? You don't want me to show Luke those pictures of you dressed up like candy corn for Halloween when you were seven because you loved those dreadful things so much? Oh, maybe you don't want me to tell him the story about when you saw the huge spider in your room, then lost sight of it and wouldn't go back in there for a month? That one is a little embarrassing, I'm sure. We'll keep that one to ourselves, Jim."

"You kind of just told him, Mom. Thanks for that." Joint laughter fills the room from their antics.

"Nice to meet you, Mr. and Mrs. Parker. And I happen to agree with you on those abominations they call candy, that taste nothing like corn." I can't tell if Luke is trying to win over my mother or not with his statement, but I agree with the sentiment as an adult. I have no idea how I thought those things were good at the time. I get nauseous just thinking of them now.

"I can see how this night is going to go already." I drop my face to my palm, knowing Luke has a similar sense of humor as my parents. I suppose that explains why I'm so comfortable around him.

"It's nice to meet you, Luke. Hope you brought your apron with you tonight. I can always use an extra set of hands in the kitchen, and from what I hear, you know your way around one." Mom is a hugger, of course, but Luke doesn't shy away, enveloping her tiny frame in his arms.

"Hey, you need to shake a man's hand before you go wrapping those arms around his wife. She might start expecting me to do this hugging thing all the time now." My father jokes like he doesn't spoil my mother in every way.

"My father is just as much of a hugger as she is—don't let him fool you."

"There he goes, giving away all your secrets, Jim. We may have to make him eat dinner on the back porch if he keeps it up."

"Luke, meet my parents, Claire and Jim Parker. Stand-up comedians. They'll be here all night."

Luke's apparent amusement at our banter makes me smile even more. "My apologies, Mr. Parker. I hope you won't hold it against me." Seeing my father shake Luke's hand does that flippy thing to my stomach.

"Okay, enough with that Mr. and Mrs. nonsense. It's Jim and Claire. Now let's go—we have some work to do in this kitchen." Mom playfully shoves my dad toward the kitchen, gesturing for Luke and me to follow them.

My parents lead the way, my dad throwing some aprons at us as soon as we enter the kitchen, while my mother starts doling out tasks for each of us. Luke is put in charge of searing the chicken breasts—which makes perfect sense. Dad just gets the menial task of watching the roasted garlic potatoes in the oven, because Mom doesn't trust him in the kitchen all that much. He'd have to survive on cereal and takeout if something ever happened to her.

"Hello, family!" Lanie's lighthearted greeting excites me until I see who's with her. When Jackson walks into the kitchen behind her, I turn to see Luke's reaction. He told me the other day that Jackson hasn't mentioned anything about us to him yet.

"Hey brother, they have you cooking already?" Jackson greets his brother without even a hint of a question in his eye, mutual backslaps exchanged.

Luke doesn't miss a beat. "Well someone has to help cook, and I know it isn't going to be you."

"Ha ha." Jackson turns my way and catches my cautious stare. "Hey, Kaden. Good to see you again."

"You, too, but stop hogging my sister for yourself." I haven't spent a lot of time around Jackson, so I make sure to smile so he knows I'm joking.

"I will when you stop hogging my brother."

"Touché." I barely have the word out when Jackson greets me as he did his brother. I see Luke smiling in my periphery over Jackson's shoulder.

We all get back to our assigned duties, our banter and laughter filling the room. It doesn't escape me how Luke and Jackson both started out silently observing before joining in with us.

Surprisingly, dinner goes smoothly without too much damage from the stories our parents tell about Lanie and me as children. Our guys even join in, telling us about the shenanigans they got up to growing up. Dakota seems to be involved in most of them, almost like a third sibling. I imagine they were all close, supporting each other through the family issues Luke told me about.

Lanie practically jumps out of her chair once she sees everyone has finished eating. "Okay, losers, let's go. Cleanup starts now. Game time is in twenty minutes. Prepare to get your asses kicked."

Lanie's bubbly personality comes with a twist—she's the biggest shit-talker when it comes to competitions of any kind. Learning from the best, she gives even my dad a run for his money.

"In your dreams! You haven't won a game in over a month. Watch the old man school you right in front of your boyfriend." Dad has no qualms about calling Lanie out. Their competitive natures are a great source of comedy in this household.

The next couple hours go by fast between the constant ribbing and debating on whose strategy is better. My father and Lanie, of course, are involved in every one of them.

I see Luke check his watch. Grabbing my phone, I notice it's already past nine, just as I get a text message from an unknown number.

> I do miss you. You know you miss me too.

My heartbeat speeds up—I have a pretty good idea who the message came from. I immediately block the number and shove it back in my pocket. When I glance back up, Luke is watching me with questioning eyes. He mouths, "You okay?"

"Wrong number, I guess." I won't be entertaining Tyler's newfound interest in me after more than a year of silence. I also don't want to worry Luke with his nonsense. He doesn't need to know all the details of what an asshole Tyler really was to me. I don't doubt he would confront Tyler about it. "We do need to get going soon, though. I have a busy day tomorrow."

We finish cleaning up the games and say our goodbyes. Jackson and Lanie walk out with us, and we all make plans to hang out at The Garden tomorrow night, since Stonewood's is closed on Mondays.

"Is everything okay?" Luke asks as soon as we get in the Jeep. "You looked upset by that text message."

"Yeah, I think it was a wrong number. I blocked it so they don't bother me again." His expression is indifferent, so I'm hoping that's the end of the subject. I probably should have told him, but I am only assuming it's Tyler. Maybe it's just a wrong number after all, in which case I'd be making a big deal out of nothing. Leaving it alone for now is best. I just wish I didn't feel like I was hiding this from Luke.

Technically, you are. He would want to know.

Chapter Twenty-Seven Part One

SOMETIMES HE'S NOT AN ANGEL

Luke

K aden was acting weird last night about the text message he received at his parents' house. I have a feeling who it was from, but I'm more concerned about Kaden's reaction. I'm glad he blocked Tyler immediately. I never doubt Kaden's fidelity—my problem with this is Tyler blatantly ignoring my warning, and Kaden worried about telling me in fear of what I'll do to Tyler. Which is a very valid fear. I may or may not have texted Jackson last night to see if there was a way to find Tyler's home or work address in the city's system. He was adamant he couldn't risk his job, even if we did have his last name, which we don't. Otherwise, I'd be scouring the internet for him. I've decided to ask Ender tonight for Tyler's last name. I hate involving him, but Tyler needs to be put in his place. I honestly don't think Ender will mind, either, given how protective he is over Kaden.

I arrive at Kaden's place to pick him up, clearing my mind before he gets in. I don't want to ruin tonight by making Kaden worry any more than he already is about all this. His anxiety must be through the roof. After I speak to Tyler, I'll tell Kaden. I hope it'll ease his mind.

"Hey, Angel. You need to stop looking so edible when we go out, or I'm going to turn into a barroom brawler fighting your admirers off," I say as Kaden gets in, his shoulders shaking with amusement.

"Who says I wouldn't want to see you go all Neanderthal in a fit of jealousy? That's kind of hot, Luke."

"Thanks for your permission to cause a scene if anyone so much as hits on you, looks at you, or even breathes on you." He shakes his head at me. I don't even have to ask for affection with Kaden as I feel the softness of his lips connect with mine. I'll never get tired of his touch. It expresses his love for me as much as his words do, both filling a void in my heart.

Having the love of my aunts growing up, and then Gabe once we met and became brothers in a sense, is different from the love Kaden shows me. I always had a feeling of something missing that I figured was due to my parents' lack of affection. Although parental love is unique in its own way, I realize now that it wasn't what I needed all along. Kaden is exactly what I needed.

We make small talk until we get to the bar where everyone has already started the first round. Gabe greets me with a beer and a smile that I know is partly because Ender is standing by his side. He keeps pretending he isn't head over heels for the guy, but I know better. Gabe the bachelor is now off the market—much to the sorrow of his fan club, which is pretty big, given his looks and larger-than-life personality. Talk about opposites attract with Ender.

"Hey, brother, glad you finally made it. You're buying the next round for being late." Gabe doles out my punishment like it wasn't going to happen anyway.

"Hey, guys. Sorry we're late. What did we miss?" Kaden asks as Connor and Faith make room on the big couch for us.

"Well, Faith and Dakota have been arguing about which series was better, The Wire or The Sopranos." Connor cups his mouth and leans into Kaden. "Which sounds more like foreplay for them if you ask me." He continues loud enough for everyone else to hear him now. "You know where Faith and I stand on that—The Wire all the way." Connor's eyes flicker closed at the obviousness of his statement. "Dakota swears by The Sopranos, insisting the psychological aspect is more interesting. Then of course you know Lanie has to throw in her two cents, saying Breaking Bad is better than both of them. Jackson obviously agrees with her because he doesn't want to be in the doghouse." He comes up for air, as he often has to with his rambling. "Lastly, Ender and Gabe are pretending to not be making heart eyes at each other, like the rest of us have no idea what's going on with them."

Everyone's eyes are on Connor in disbelief, even though we know he has zero filter.

"What?" Feigning innocence with a smile, he wraps his arm around Kaden, pulling him into his side for a hug, and kisses his cheek. Even though I know they're only friends, I can't say I'm not feeling jealous when I grab his waist and pull him back toward me.

Kaden and Connor's heads both whip around to face me. "My, my hasn't someone gotten a little possessive of his man? Nothing turns me on more than a little 'he's mine' behavior. If Kaden wasn't my best friend, I'd be dragging you out the door already."

"Connor is being Connor times a hundred today, if anyone hasn't noticed." Ender shakes his head at his friend as we all laugh and settle back into conversation, moving things away from Connor's unbridled candor.

We're on our second round of drinks when I hear, "Oh my goodness. Hi, Dr. Parker." I glance up and see Kelsey, Kaden's assistant, and a stocky guy almost twice her size standing next to the couch. "Oh, and Mr. Stonewood, nice to see you again." The playful tone lets me know Kaden hasn't divulged his personal life to her much since we met. I'm surprised she hasn't hammered him with questions about me, considering she's obviously invested in Kaden's happiness.

"Hi, Kelsey. Nice to see you out of work. You don't have to call me Doctor here, though. Kaden is fine." She beams with excitement.

"Hi, Kelsey. The name's Luke, by the way." I reach out to shake her companion's hand. "Hey man, nice to meet you. You want to join us?"

He checks with Kelsey as he shakes my hand before responding, "Yeah, sounds good. Austin, nice to meet everyone." He gives a small wave to the group.

I grab Kaden's waist and drag him onto my lap. "Have a seat, guys, there's enough room here." Connor scoots over to make more room for them between us. Kaden has no qualms with where I positioned him, turning sideways so he can see me.

"Thanks for letting us join. Our friends cancelled last minute, so it's just us." Kelsey sits next to Kaden and me while Austin slides in next to Connor, who is overtly curious about the couple. I can see he's going to have a hard time controlling his thoughts already. He starts playing a game of 20 Questions with the couple, hogging their attention. They don't appear to mind, though, seeming happy to be included.

When conversations within the group resume, I start to regret having Kaden sit on my lap. Every miniscule movement he makes, his ass rubs against my dick, and it's getting hard to ignore. I squeeze his waist once when I can tell his last shift was purposeful. He's completely aware of what he's doing.

"Does anyone want some food? I need some fries." I volunteer to order at the bar for everyone, hoping to get out of the position I put myself in. Kaden climbs off me, glancing down to see that he accomplished his goal. He's gentleman enough to help by walking in front of me, staying close enough to hide my half-hard cock.

Approaching the bar, I wrap my arm around Kaden, palm on his stomach, pinning him between my body and the edge. I lean in until his hair is brushing my eyelashes, and his intoxicating cologne I've grown to crave fills my olfactory nerves. "You're going to regret that when your ass is as red as a raspberry," I warn him, not caring if anyone overhears us. Apparently, Kaden is dead set on being mischievous tonight, and pushes his ass back into my groin. Retaliating, I gently sink my teeth into his neck as the bearded bartender from the previous time we were here turns toward us.

Kaden doesn't see him in time, and they speak over each other. "Will it be your hand or you plowing your cock into me that's turning my ass red?"

"Hey welcome back, gentlemen. What can I get you?" The bartender laughs as he overhears Kaden.

"Look at that, he called me a gentleman," Kaden teases before ordering the food and a couple drinks.

"I think he was just being nice, Angel. Gentlemen don't cocktease while in a crowded bar."

"It's not teasing when you offer yourself openly for the taking." Kaden glances over his shoulder, his eyes on mine as every inch of my skin sets ablaze.

The bartender comes back with our drinks, once again catching Kaden and me in a heated moment. "Here you go, guys. Your food should be out shortly."

I turn his way, extending my hand to him. "I'm Luke, and this is Kaden. Nice to meet you, man."

"Bryce, nice to meet you guys." Kaden follows my lead, shaking Bryce's hand.

"Bryce, is there any way you can have a server deliver our drinks and food over there to our friends? We have to make a pit stop in the restroom."

Bryce shakes his head, grinning. "Yeah, no problem. I'd need a moment of privacy after that, too." His audible amusement fades into the background as he walks away.

Kaden rotates his body to face mine. "I don't have to go to the restroom, Bug."

"Neither do I, Angel." I grasp Kaden's hand and steer us toward the front door, out to the parking lot.

"Where are you taking me?" Quietly laughing with excitement as he walks across the lot, Kaden doesn't object to my manhandling.

Looking for some privacy, I'm thankful I backed into a parking space earlier that has a fence and building directly behind it. I steer us to the rear of the Jeep, pinning Kaden against it, his back to my chest. The darkness of the night cloaks us enough to remain unseen and Kaden braces himself with his hands next to his head. I don't waste any time undoing his jeans and reaching in to wrap my hand around his hard cock, glad to see I wasn't the only one affected by his impishness.

"Did I ever tell you that I love every side of your personality? When you take control of me in the bedroom, I don't think my cock has ever been that hard before." I slowly stroke him, my confessions flowing from me like an open faucet that can't be shut off. "The way you got nervous when we first met and still do when you're out of your comfort zone." My lips explore his neck between my words. "But the way you purposely and unapologetically turn me on in public damn near makes me lose my mind every time." As my grip tightens around him, the sharp intake of air into Kaden's lungs makes my cock ache even more.

I spit on my fingers before sliding my free hand down the back of his pants, resting my middle finger in his crease and applying soft pressure to his hole. "Is your hole hungry? Does it need to be filled? Is that why you're determined to tease me and get my cock hard, hoping I'd bend you over a table and fuck you in a room full of people?"

His heavy breaths as I push my finger harder against him have me picking up the pace of my strokes. He widens his stance, giving me permission to use his body. Letting go of his cock, I reach down behind his balls to massage his taint, alternating the pressure against it while I slip my middle finger inside him from behind.

Kaden starts to moan, low and sinful, the sounds getting louder and louder. "You need to be a little quieter, Angel. You don't want an audience, do you? You don't want anyone to see me abusing your hole right here in the parking lot, do you? Maybe I need to make you put a fist in your mouth? We already know that works, don't we?" With every pump, my finger inches farther inside him, making obscenities spill from his lips, filling my ears with a symphony of want. I don't know who this is punishing more—Kaden or me.

"I need you inside me, now," he begs me, breathless and panting. I have no willpower to deny him.

Chapter Twenty-Seven Part Two

Playing in Public is Our Thing

Kaden

I'm not too proud to beg. Luke is driving me crazy between his hands double-teaming me and his mouth that won't tame what comes out of it, but I'm not complaining. I just need more, or I think I might spontaneously combust.

Luke slowly pulls his hands away from me. I hear him rustling behind me, and when I look over my shoulder I see him take a packet of lube out of his wallet. My adrenaline soars even higher as I start sliding my jeans lower as he prepares himself. His cold, wet fingers enter me again without warning. I can't find it in me to care if anyone can see us. Instead, I arch my back and push my ass up toward him farther to give him better access.

Luke withdraws his hand and positions his cock against me. Leaning my head on the Jeep, I spread my ass cheeks to help him as he enters me in slow thrusts. He grabs my chin, arching my neck backward to fuse his mouth to mine, our tongues embracing each other. The gentleness with which he's loving my body right now doesn't fit his commanding behavior a few minutes ago. His mouth, hot and insistent against mine, captures every sound that tries to escape me as overwhelming pleasure consumes my body and mind.

I cup the back of his head, grasping his hair to break our kiss. "I love you, Luke."

"I love you, Kaden," Luke sighs, then rests his forehead against my shoulder as his slow thrusts accelerate.

If my neglected cock could jump for joy, it would when Luke spits in his hand and wraps his fist around me again. The moan that leaves me is so loud that someone has to have heard, but my mind is too scattered with pleasure right now to control myself. Luke's arm around my waist tightens as he pulls me in closer, pushing himself deeper into me. Wrapping one arm around him, I hold his ass against me with my palm to still him for a moment. His stroking continues, pushing me closer to the edge. Then the short, leisurely pumping against my ass resumes, sending my mind spinning like a cyclone.

"I need to come, Luke. Please."

"Anything you need, I'll give you, Angel," Luke whispers, then keeps true to his word like I knew he would.

His hand that was around my waist now grasps my throat as he places one last kiss on me. All gentleness is gone when his carnal side, which I've come to enjoy so much, comes out to play, the slapping of skin on skin echoing in my ears. "Fuck, yeah. Just like that." My words come out in more of a broken whine than complete words. His hand, stroking and twisting around my cock, combined with the hammering my hole is taking, makes my knees weak. I would be on the ground by now if his hand on my throat and the Jeep weren't holding me upright.

"Baby, come now. I can't hold out any longer." Luke begging me to come has its desired effect as my cock erupts all over his hand. The muscles of my ass clench around his cock, and with one final thrust I feel his warmth spreading inside of me, his sweaty body trembling against mine.

As our panting begins to slow down and my brain returns to normal functioning, I hear my phone incessantly dinging with messages in my pants that are still around my ankles.

"Shit, that's probably one of them yelling at us for leaving without saying goodbye," I huff out with barely enough breath.

"They'll forgive us. Especially Connor if we tell him why." Luke laughs at his own joke.

"You're wrong—he'll be madder we didn't ask him to join, or at least let him watch."

Luke bites my neck before pulling out of me. "Don't even joke about that. No one gets to touch you or watch me fuck you—ever. You got that?" He emphasizes his statement with a whack to my ass that makes me jump. I won't disagree with him, but if egging him on gives me that response, I'm all for it.

We finish cleaning ourselves up and get dressed, although I can still feel his cum dripping out of me when we get in the Jeep to leave. I must admit, it's a feeling I enjoy more than I ever thought I would. You won't ever find me complaining about it. I'm glad he is the first—and hopefully the only—man I ever let fuck me bare.

Only, Kaden? That sounds like a forever to me.

The ride back to his place is peacefully quiet, Luke's palm never leaving my thigh. I'm deeply satiated, and I want to pass out for the night. I didn't realize I closed my eyes until I feel Luke's hand squeeze my thigh. "We're home, babe. I would carry you, but I don't think I'd make it all the way inside my apartment without dropping you." We laugh together at the imagery. He kisses me softly before we exit the Jeep, then we're strolling into his building and up to his floor. Of course, as soon as he opens his apartment door, the shrill meowing of an overdramatic Fred, who thinks he's starving but in reality ate about four hours ago, fills the room. I give him a little scruff loving before I make a beeline to the bedroom, only taking off my shoes before collapsing on the bed.

I faintly hear Luke stepping into the room, then he begins tenderly undressing me. Lying down next to me, he pulls me into him, and the warmth of his skin pressed to mine soon has me drifting off. The last thing I remember hearing is my phone dinging a few more times.

Chapter Twenty-Eight

NOT THE MORNING I EXPECTED TO HAVE

Luke

I wake to my phone screaming at me to pick it up. I finally get to it after the fifth ring. "This better be important." I check the time on the phone and see it's nearing seven in the morning.

"Any time I call, it's important, and don't you forget that, mister." G's voice is never bothersome to hear, even this early.

"How could I ever forget?" I can't help but laugh with her.

"Did I interrupt any hanky-panky with that handsome guy of yours?"

"That's none of your business, G, but no, you didn't."

"Darn, next time I'll wait an hour longer." I hear her fingers snap in the background.

"G, is there a reason you called me at the butt crack of dawn?" Kaden groans next to me, obviously annoyed at being woken up so early.

"Your aunt's birthday is coming up next week. Make sure all you kids get here for the BBQ."

Damn it, I almost forgot about the party. "We'll be there. I'll make sure everyone comes."

"Okay. Just an FYI—your parents will be here, too."

Wonderful. That should be fun. "It's not a problem. I can manage for a day. I always have, right?" I tell her.

"Alright, kiddo. I'll talk with you later. I love you." G never forgets to tell me.

"Love you, G."

"You're too loud," Kaden's sleepy voice comes out muffled from under the covers.

"Sorry, G called and wanted to make sure we were all coming to Brenda's birthday BBQ next weekend. I'm sorry I forgot to tell you, but if you don't come with me, I think G might send out a search party for you."

"Of course, now shush and go back to sleep." Kaden's days of early rising to run have gotten less and less over the past month. I think he likes cuddling more than running at this point.

I'm proven right when he climbs on top of me and wraps his body around mine, koala bear style. His head rests on my chest, his shaggy morning hair tickling my chin.

"I can hear you thinking. It's so loud it echoes in the room. What's going on?" Kaden must sense the tension in my body.

"I haven't seen my father in more than a year. He wasn't home the last two times I went to visit them. He and my mother are going to be at Brenda and G's house next week."

"Are you worried about seeing him in general, or about me? I'm figuring he doesn't know anything about us, since you haven't seen them." He says the last part as a statement more than a question.

"Yeah, it's not like I really talk to either of my parents besides the occasional text or call with my mother to let her know I'm still alive." Kaden's lips brush my chest, and it relaxes me enough to continue. "Those always go the same way—she gives me the third degree about when I'm getting married and giving her grandbabies."

"That sounds like so much fun. She's going to love me." He sighs, and I can already tell his anxiety is going to be through the roof at the BBQ.

"Nothing either of my parents say will matter when it comes to us. I don't want you worrying about that." Kaden gives a half-nod against my chest as I tighten my arms around him.

Before he starts to relax too much, I nudge him to get moving. "No more sleeping. You need to start getting ready for work. I'm going to make us a quick breakfast."

He gives one last groan, presses a hasty kiss to my lips, then rolls off me and the bed onto his feet. He grabs some clothes from the couple drawers I cleaned out for him since he's been staying over a few times a week now, and heads for the bathroom. "Good, because I'm starving. We never got to eat the food we ordered last night at the bar."

"If someone would behave themselves in public, then we wouldn't have missed eating now, would we?"

Kaden replies in his singsong tone, "If someone would stop rewarding me with his cock every time I misbehave, then I wouldn't have a reason to now, would I?" I throw a pillow at him just as he makes it to the doorway.

Fred's starving wail drowns out Kaden's amused shriek as he runs into the bathroom. "Go feed that poor thing, or I'll call the ASPCA on you," he yells as he shuts the door behind him.

Feeling like Kaden deserves a dose of his own medicine, I get ready to cook breakfast in the most unconventional way that I possibly can.

When he arrives in the kitchen a little while later, I'm in front of the stove frying bacon, bare naked except for my full-coverage apron. The lack of reaction I get is not what I was hoping for, though. Kaden is staring down at his phone, wide-eyed, scrolling.

"What's going on?"

He looks up at me like he didn't expect me to be there. Instead of answering, he hands me his phone. When I see that the messages app on his screen is filled with incoming messages from an unknown number, I scroll to the beginning of the chat that started last night.

> Nice show you just put on for the world to see.

> Since when did you start having sex in public?

> First a bathroom stall in a club. Now the middle of a parking lot.

> Were you always a little whore?

> If you had told me you liked this sort of thing, I would've taken you out in public more often.

> I won't lie and say I didn't miss seeing the face you make as you're coming.

> You never let me fuck you raw before. We're going to have to correct that sooner rather than later.

I feel my temperature rise the more I read on. The next set of messages came in about thirty minutes later.

> Sleeping at your boyfriend's house. Guess I'll have to plan a visit another time.

> See you soon, Kaden.

"What the fuck? How did he know where we were last night? And the night we met? How long has he been following you?" My thoughts are circling like a tornado in my head. Imagining Tyler stalking Kaden, watching us together, has me spiraling. Instead of giving in to my emotions, I call the number the text messages came from.

"What are you doing? Don't call him, Luke. Please, you're just asking for trouble."

The call immediately goes to a generic recording, stating the number is no longer in service.

"What do you mean 'asking for trouble,' Kaden? You never said anything about Tyler behaving any way remotely close to this."

Kaden stares at me in silence. Turning off the burners on the stove, I take his hand and lead him to the bedroom. I can't have a serious conversation with him when I'm naked in an apron.

I throw clothes on while Kaden sits on the bed with his eyes closed, fiddling with his fingers. Climbing onto the bed behind him, I wrap my arms and legs around him and pull him in close to my chest.

Attempting to control my anger at Tyler, I rest my chin on Kaden's shoulder. "Kaden, what's going on? Talk to me."

"Tyler wasn't always the nicest of guys."

"Tell me everything." I'm on full alert now, ready to find Tyler without even knowing the whole story yet.

"It wasn't that bad. He has a temper, especially when he's jealous. He can be controlling." Kaden rolls his head back to rest on my shoulder, his eyes still closed. "Everything was always his way or nothing. I told you I believed all his reasoning for keeping us a secret, but it was more like mind games. I see that in hindsight."

The moment of silence is deafening as I wait for Kaden to gather his thoughts. Obviously, a lot of emotions are flowing through him right now.

"Every time I would start to pull away, he knew exactly what to do to make me stay. He would make me feel loved and important. Then, once I was comfortable with our arrangement again, he went back to being a jerk. He was always right, and nothing I said mattered. It was a vicious cycle."

"Kaden, did he ever hurt you, physically?" The words leave my lips like poison, stinging them. His answer won't determine if, but rather how bad, I hurt Tyler.

"I wouldn't say he hurt me. Did he scare me sometimes? Yes. Any time a guy talked to me too long or maybe flirted with me in front of him, he'd wait until we were alone, and then harass me about it. A couple times, he pushed me up against the wall and would grab my jaw, making me look at him while he scolded me like it was my fault. I was never allowed to hang out with those guys ever again, even though I told him I had no interest in them."

My mind races back to Kaden in the restaurant and the desperate look he gave me when Tyler had him against the wall. He must've been terrified.

"He tried to get me to stop being friends with Ender and Connor so many times, but that was a hard line for me. I always stood my ground on that demand. Instead of forcing me in some other way, he would just be an asshole to them so they wouldn't want to hang out with us." Kaden lets out a small laugh. "He underestimated their love for me. That just made them hang around us even more. They hated him so much. I wish I would've listened to their warnings sooner. It would've saved me a lot of time and heartache."

"Where does he live, Kaden?"

Kaden turns around to face me, mimicking my arms and legs around him. "Please don't do anything stupid. I don't want you getting hurt—or worse, getting arrested for hurting him."

181

"Kaden, where does he live?" I stare directly into his eyes, letting him know how serious I am about this.

"I don't know, Luke. He got married and disappeared from my life. I let it be. I wasn't going to interact with him ever again. Ender and Connor wouldn't have let me if I tried."

"Where does he work?"

"Luke, please." Kaden rests his forehead against mine.

I don't want to give in. Tyler is not going to get away with any of this, but I also don't want to upset and worry Kaden.

"We're changing your phone number, today. I won't bend on that." I compromise, at least through his eyes.

He kisses me softly. "Thank you for wanting to protect me."

"There's no 'wanting' needed in that sentence. I protect what's mine." He doesn't need to know how far I'll go for that—at least, not yet.

Fred decides this is the perfect time to interrupt, wedging himself between us but favoring Kaden, of course. He all but forgets me when Kaden is around.

We leave the conversation at that and go about getting ready for work. I know I have a phone call to make once Kaden leaves, though.

Brenda's Birthday BBQ

I've been indifferent to seeing my parents since G told me they would be here today, until we pull up to Brenda and G's house for the BBQ. Now, my stomach decides to cramp with nervousness. I grab the bottle of wine from the back seat and get out before I have a chance to change my mind.

"You sure you're okay with this? Brenda and G will understand if it's too much." I think Kaden senses the tension in my hand when I grasp his for support.

"I'm fine. I don't want to make a big deal out of this." He sees right through me, squeezing my hand.

Walking into the backyard, Kaden drops his hand, probably worried my parents are already here.

"We're not doing that, ever." I wrap my hand around his once more, kissing the back of it for reassurance. I know he wants to make this day as easy as possible for me, but I refuse to make him uncomfortable or hide our relationship for them.

"Kaden!" I've been shoved to the back burner by G now too, as she runs to greet him with that powerful hug of hers.

"I've been forgotten already," I tease her, ready for the snarky comeback.

"I talk to you every other day. You don't need special treatment." She finally decides to share the love, practically squeezing the life out of me.

"G, you've called Kaden almost every day this week to make sure he was still coming. He spent almost an hour talking with you on Monday night."

"Leave her alone. She can call me as much as she wants. Green doesn't look good on you, Bug."

"Great, now I'm being ganged up on. Why am I here again?"

"Maybe to see your parents, since it's so hard to visit them at home." The deep voice that joins the conversation instantly has me taking a sharp breath. I still don't understand why I have that reaction every time I hear my father's voice.

"Hey, Dad. How's it going?" I offer my hand to him, knowing a hug is never a greeting he partakes in.

"Same as it's always been. About to retire in a few months. That's the perk of being an officer. Early retirement instead of working your entire life."

The dig at me not following the family tradition of career choice doesn't escape me.

"That's good to hear. I'm glad you're happy with your career choice, as am I."

His grimace confirms I hit the mark I aimed for. He glances at Kaden and down to our connected hands. When his eyes return to mine, I see exactly what I expected—displeased judgement.

"Hey, Pop, good to see you." Jackson's timing couldn't have been planned more perfectly. The poor guy still has hope for the affection we've never received when he comes between us, attempting to give our father a hug. He gets a friendly tap on the shoulder from him when he turns toward the rest of the partygoers behind him, walking away with only a "hey, son" in return. Jackson stands silently as he watches his father leave him like he was a stranger on the street. I will never understand how clueless he is to how much emotional damage he has done to us.

"C'mon boys, let's go find a beer and some food." G links her arms with Jackson and me and walks further into the backyard. Kaden and Lanie stick by our sides, their attention never wavering from us.

My mother approaches us, giving me a soft hug and peck on the cheek, which has me immediately questioning her motives.

"Hi, Mom. Nice to see you."

"Hello, my boy. Glad you could make it. It's been too long." She smiles half-heartedly.

"And who might this be?" Her question, aimed at Kaden, makes me brace for her reaction—whatever it is, I'll have to be tactful, so as to not start trouble at Brenda's party.

"Mom, this is Kaden, my partner."

"Oh, I didn't know you and Gabe took on another partner for the restaurant. When did that happen?" I can tell her feigned ignorance is just a prompt for me to explain further.

"No, Mom. Kaden is my partner—as in a loving, committed personal relationship."

"Nice to meet you, Kaden." Her nodding and addressing Kaden doesn't surprise me. She doesn't like being perceived as blatantly rude.

"Alright, enough of the pleasantries. Give your aunt a birthday hug, and let's get some grub." Brenda takes the moment to break up the awkwardness between us.

"Happy Birthday, Brenda." Kaden hugs Brenda like they're old friends, and I can't help smiling at his obvious disregard for my parents, yet he lovingly greets my aunts. I'm not the only one who notices, either, by the looks on some of the faces around us.

I greet Brenda then clasp my hand around Kaden's, walking to meet with our group of friends that arrived before us, not sparing any more of my attention on my parents. Brenda and G join us in support.

As expected, our friends ignore everything they just saw, carrying on with their conversations as we join in seamlessly. These people have become more important to me than I ever thought possible. From our outings at The Garden, to the nights we just sit around one of our apartments, we've all grown close over the past couple months. Even moody Ender and I have been getting along well.

The backyard starts to fill up with some of my aunts' friends. Dakota's parents show up at some point without any of us noticing, including Dakota. Maybe because Faith is paying attention to him today and looks like she's actually enjoying his company, instead of the usual tension between them.

"I'm going to get a drink." Kaden sneaks up on my side, startling me. " Do you want another?" He'd disappeared with Lanie and G a little while ago, and I'd been wondering where they'd all gone off to.

"Hey, babe." I softly peck his lips. "Yeah, I'll come with you." We link hands and head for the beverage table and coolers.

I tense up a little when I see my uncle standing by the beer cooler, talking to someone. I try not to make eye contact—I'd rather not talk to him, so I don't have to bother pretending to like talking to him.

"What do you want? Beer, water, or a real drink?" Kaden asks at the same time as we hear, "Luke, how's it going? You haven't been around in a while."

"Hi, Jack. Nice to see you." I put on the best fake smile I can stomach.

"What's going on up in the city life for you?" Jack eyes Kaden curiously without introducing himself, which doesn't surprise me at all.

"My new restaurant opened last month. It's doing really well."

"Yeah, looks like a bunch of new things happening up there, huh?" He looks from Kaden to our hands, then finally looks at me.

The average person would react differently than I feel the need to in this situation. Instead, I don't grant him the reaction he's looking for—or any for that matter. Instead, I pass Kaden's hand to my free one, and move my other hand to his back. "Let's get that drink." I guide Kaden to the other side of the table without responding to Jack at all. He isn't worth the time or effort—for many reasons. Any attempt to educate him would fall on deaf ears. I won't subject Kaden to any of his behavior, either.

We grab our drinks and are able to walk away without Jack bothering us further. "I don't want to tell you to ignore his bigotry, because I know you might be experiencing it for the first time today. I don't want to invalidate anything you're feeling, either. Do you need or want to talk about it now or later?" Kaden knows the right things to say, and I couldn't love him any more than I do in this moment.

"No need. His opinion means nothing to me. Let's enjoy the rest of the day."

Chapter Twenty-Nine Part One

ONE THING ALWAYS LEADS TO ANOTHER

Kaden

While it might look like Luke is attempting to have fun, acting like nothing's wrong as we socialize with everyone else, I know him better than that—and I know he can't keep this up forever. Every chance I get, I offer him gentle touches; subtle acts of comfort to remind him that I'm here for him. That I'm ready to talk about it as soon as he is.

The moment comes when Luke suddenly clasps my hand and leads me inside the house. When we stop in the empty kitchen, he wraps his arms around me and rests his forehead on my shoulder.

"Bug, talk to me."

"I'm trying not to think about them and their bullshit, but I keep catching them looking at us. I truly don't care what they think. I'm just trying not to ruin the party by telling them how I feel about them and how they treat us all. I've always been too scared to tell them how I really feel. For once in my life, I'm finding it very hard to keep my mouth shut."

"You need to relax a little. As much as I'd love to see you tell them off, now is not the time or place." I massage his shoulders, attempting to loosen the knots that have formed. It doesn't seem to be helping much, though.

I look around and see that no one is in the house. Thinking of a quick solution—or I at least hope it will be—I lift his head and kiss him softly.

"C'mon," I say as I lead Luke to the bathroom down the hallway.

"Babe, what are you doing?" Luke questions with a smile, knowing damn well what I am up to.

"You can't relax on your own, so I'll make it happen my way. Get in there." I nudge him into the bathroom, closing and locking the door behind us.

"You're going to get us in trouble. If G finds us in here, she'll never let us live it down." Luke frames my face with his hands, kissing me between words.

"Stop pretending to object and close your mouth before someone hears us." I push him against the wall and drop to my knees.

There's no time for playing here. I have one goal in mind, and it's to get him to relax. I unfasten his jeans and release his dick, stroking his shaft to get him fully hard. His hand caresses the back of my head when I put him in my mouth. Staring up at him, his tender gaze makes my heart swell. This isn't about getting off, and he knows it. I'd do anything to ease his pain.

I work quickly, our eyes remaining connected the whole time. When I feel him getting closer, I fondle his balls, hoping to give him one last push off the cliff. He grasps my hair and holds my face close to his groin. His cock pulses, emptying his cum down my throat while he bites his lower lip to silence himself.

I clean him up before rising from my knees. His head is against the wall, and I kiss his chin as I lean all my weight against him. When he squeezes me back just as hard, I know this was exactly what he needed.

"Feel a little better?"

"Yeah, a lot. Thank you." His lips find mine in a passion-filled kiss.

"I love you, Kaden."

"I love you, and I would love to stay in here by ourselves all day, but people are going to start noticing we're gone soon. You ready to go back out there?"

He nods, fastening his jeans back up. Unfortunately, I open the door to see Luke's father coming down the hallway toward us.

He stops in his tracks, watching us leave the bathroom together. Luke's hands hold my hips from behind me as we attempt to walk past him.

"Is that what you do now? Leave family functions to do God knows what in a bathroom with him?"

Luke's hands tighten on my hips seemingly from the disdain in his father's voice when he said 'him,' then suddenly they're gone.

Fuck!

I swing around, quickly grabbing Luke's arm to pull him back toward me. This is not going to end well.

Chapter Twenty-Nine Part Two

CAN YOUR HEART BREAK FROM SOMETHING IT NEVER HAD?

Luke

K aden attempts to stop me, but it's pointless. I'm done biting my tongue for this man.

"Him? You have the balls to say anything to me about who I choose to love? This man has shown me more love in the few months he *chose* to be in my life than you have in the thirty years since you and your wife brought me into this world. Do you not see who you are? What you've done to your sons? Jackson still begs for you to show him an ounce of attention—love, affection, *anything*! But you treat him like a stranger. No, fuck that, you treat strangers better than you treat your own sons. Now you want to act holier than thou because I found someone who shows me more love than you ever could, but he's a man, so that's a problem for you. Nothing I do will ever be good enough for you, will it?

Unless I live by your rules, right? How about this: stay the fuck out of my life. I've never felt love from you before, and I sure as fuck don't need it now. Do you see that group of people out there? Those friends of ours are more of a family to me than you and your wife have ever been. So, let's stop pretending to be a family, because I don't fucking need either of you." Face-to-face, I stare down my father, daring him to say something while I catch my breath.

His wide-eyed stare doesn't change. After a few seconds, I turn around and take Kaden's hand, and we start to walk away. I only make it a couple feet before noticing the crowd we've attracted at the back door, my mother included.

She stands there with tears in her eyes and her hand over her mouth. It doesn't affect me as I thought it would when I imagined this moment in the past, and I'm not sorry for it.

"You should have done better," I say to her as I look over her shoulder to Brenda and G adding, "I'm sorry we ruined the party. I'll call you later." They're in the same state as my mother, which hurts my heart more than anything else.

I lead Kaden away from them without looking back. My adrenaline is pumping too hard right now. "Can you drive, please?" I ask Kaden, handing him my rattling keys.

"Of course." He holds my hands still for a moment, until I nod to let him know I'm okay.

The drive back to my apartment is silent. Kaden doesn't ask unnecessary questions right now, and its appreciated. My mind is spinning so fast it's giving me a headache. I rest my head on the window and close my eyes, hoping it doesn't get any worse.

Kaden gets us home in no time, gently helping me out and up into my apartment. I head straight to the bedroom, kicking off my shoes and getting under the covers. Fred is next to me in seconds, like his emotional radar honed in on me. I wrap an arm around him and pull him in close.

I feel the bed sink behind me, then Kaden's body is pressed up against mine, and all the tension seeps out of my body in his embrace.

I've never fallen asleep so fast in my life.

Chapter Thirty

PICKING UP THE PIECES OF HIM

Kaden

I look at my watch and see its about 2 a.m. when Luke starts to stir. Neither myself nor Fred have left his side. He rolls onto his back, rubbing the sleep from his eyes. I pass him the water I put on the nightstand earlier.

"Do you want to talk about it? You don't have to, but I'm here if you do."

He passes the glass back to me, collapsing on the bed again. "I don't know what to talk about. I fucked up Brenda's day."

"And?" I push a little, knowing there's more.

"And what? There isn't anything else. I didn't lose anything today." He goes silent for a moment. "I take that back. I lost my anger I've been holding onto for so long. I unloaded what I've been carrying around most of my life." He keeps his eyes closed while he lets it all out. "I was shocked and totally overtaken by adrenaline afterward. I meant every word I said, and I don't regret any of it. I'm just hoping Brenda and G will forgive me for ruining their party."

"Luke, they're not upset with you. They were hurting *for* you. I saw it in their faces. And you are not to take the blame for ruining the party.

Your father and uncle have the sole responsibility of that—for what they did there, and in the past."

Luke doesn't respond. I wrap myself around him, offering comfort until he's ready. I assume he's falling back asleep when we lie in silence for a bit, until he startles me.

"I need to take a shower." He taps my arms, motioning for me to unravel myself from his body. Rolling over onto my back, I watch him hurriedly get up and walk into the bathroom.

I hear the shower turn on and debate whether I should let him be or join in case he needs me. I don't argue with myself long. I know I wouldn't want to be alone if I were in his place, so I won't let him do this on his own.

When I open the shower door, Luke has his forearms crossed on the shower wall in front of him, his forehead resting against them, and piping hot water cascading down his body. Getting in behind him, I arch my body over his back, scooping my arms under his, and placing my palms flat on his chest.

I can't stop my tears when Luke's body starts jerking, the sounds of his sobbing bouncing off the walls. I tighten my grip around him, applying as much pressure as I possibly can in this position. When Luke's knees start to bend, I attempt to hold us upright, but I give up, knowing it's a losing battle. I slide us to the floor as gently as possible, turning Luke around to rest his head against my chest as he unleashes the emotions he's kept bottled up inside for years. With his arms locked around my waist, I think about how proud I am of this man for finally being able to tell his parents how he really feels.

We lie there on the shower floor until the water starts to run cold. Luke's breathing has returned back to normal, but he still hasn't spoken a single word.

"C'mon, Bug. I need to get you out of here before we freeze to death." He complies without a word while I help him to his feet.

I dry us off quickly while Luke leans into the counter with his hands against the sink's edge, head bowed between his arms. I steer him to the bed and get us under the covers, where Luke hangs an arm and leg over my body, his face nuzzled against my collarbone.

"I love you, Luke," I whisper as I kiss his wet hair.

"Thank you." His voice is barely audible, but I know those two words mean everything in this moment.

I reluctantly went to work today. When Luke woke up, he basically forced me to go, insisting that he was fine, saying that I shouldn't mess up my schedule. I protested at first, but when I realized he wasn't going to budge on the matter, I compromised. I had Kelsey reschedule some of my morning appointments to early evening tonight, while leaving my afternoon appointments unchanged.

I'm sure Kelsey can sense that something is going on, but thankfully, she doesn't hammer me with questions. By the time I finish with everyone on the books, it's about 5:30 p.m.. When I get back to my office, I check my phone again to make sure I didn't miss any messages from Luke. Instead, I find almost a dozen texts from another unknown number. It's obvious right away that they're from Tyler. They started coming in about an hour ago, and they've been getting more and more threatening.

> you think changing your number will make me go away? It's a lot easier to find a phone number than you think Kaden

or did your little boyfriend make you do it?

maybe he should mind his own fucking business

you were fine before you met him

you don't need him Kaden. just stay away from him

I will hurt him if I need to

is that what I need to do to get you to leave him?

you don't belong to him

you'll be sorry you ever met him I promise you that

I hit call on Luke's number with shaking fingers. When it just rings with no answer, I grab my keys, practically running out of the door without so much as a word to Kelsey.

I have tunnel vision as I make my way to my car, dialing Luke's number over and over again. I'm so preoccupied that I don't see someone come up behind me until it's too late. Not until I'm pinned to my driver's door by a body pressed hard against my back and a large hand tight around my neck.

"Where are you off to so quickly, Kaden? In a rush to make sure he's okay?" Tyler's menacing tone throws my mind into a panic—so much worse than it was already.

"What do you want, Tyler? Why are you doing this?"

"Why? I told you before—no one gets to have you. Not then, not now. Your little boy toy is no exception."

I think back to those times he was in a jealous rage, remembering those exact words that didn't seem as important back then as they do right now.

"Tyler, what are you talking about? You were the one who left me. You wanted nothing to do with me. You got married. Why all of a sudden am I so important to you?"

"You think me walking into that asshole's restaurant that night was a coincidence?"

His sinister laugh at his admission makes my stomach turn. His grip on my neck tightens, and I cry out in pain.

"Leave him. Tell him you're done, or next time it won't be your parking lot I show up in."

Before I can respond, Tyler is ripped off me from behind. I spin around, finding Tyler being shoved away from me by Austin, stumbling to regain his balance. Austin puts himself between Tyler and me, like a barrier, and I'm thankful that Austin is a bigger guy knowing Tyler won't be able to overpower him.

"Kaden, are you okay?" Austin asks, not taking his eyes off Tyler.

"Another guard dog, Kaden? You fucking this one too?"

"I don't know who you are, asshole, but you better walk away before you see how hard this dog bites."

I massage my neck as Tyler gets up. "See you soon, Kaden." Tyler retreats to the other side of the parking lot, and we both watch him until his car disappears.

Austin turns to me with concerned eyes. "Are you okay? Who was that guy?" I hear Kelsey approach, asking the same question, having caught the end of the confrontation.

"Thank you, Austin. I'm okay. He scared me more than anything. Can I explain later? I really need to get home and make sure Luke is okay," I say as quickly as possible.

"Dr. Parker, please be careful," Kelsey pleads.

I nod as I get into my car and speed out of the parking lot.

I call Jackson on the way to Luke's place and tell him everything. He doesn't seem as surprised as I thought he would, something that makes sense when he confesses to Luke having called him a week or so ago, asking him to get information on Tyler from the city's system. Jackson apologizes after that, saying he refused because he didn't want to lose his job. By the time I pull into Luke's apartment parking lot, Jackson is already on his way over.

I choose to take the three flights of stairs, knowing it'll be faster than waiting for that slow elevator. Barreling through the door of Luke's apartment, I see him wide-eyed, standing with wet hair and a towel around his waist in front of the fridge. I'm panting as I slam into his body, sending us stumbling backward into the counter.

"Kaden, what the fuck?" He drops the water bottle from his hand, closing his arms around me. "What happened? What's going on?"

My breathing is erratic from taking the stairs or the sheer panic in the last thirty minutes, either way I can't focus on anything but Luke, safe in my arms.

"Angel, please tell me something, anything."

I don't reply. I couldn't even if I tried. We just stand there in a tense embrace until Jackson rushes through the open door.

"Fuck, you're okay. Geez, I've never been so scared in my life." I can hear Jackson huffing behind me—most likely from taking the stairs, as well.

"Will someone please tell me what the hell is going on here?"

I don't let go of Luke, letting Jackson explain instead, knowing there's no way I could do it right now. Luke's arms have me in a death grip as the story goes on. When Jackson is finished telling him everything, Luke grasps my biceps, gently pulling me off him.

"Angel, did he hurt you? Are you okay? Tell me, please."

I nod when his hands cup my face. "I'm okay—I was just terrified he did something to you. You weren't answering your phone, and I wasn't paying attention in the parking lot when he came up behind me. Then Austin showed up out of nowhere, and I don't even remember anything on the way here besides calling Jackson. I may have blown a few red lights."

"A few traffic violations are the least of my worries. If something were to happen to you..." He engulfs me in his arms again. Then, Jackson and Luke start to discuss what to do about Tyler. Jackson says there isn't much we can do based on the information we have so far. I could press charges over him putting his hands on me in the parking lot, he says, but even that wouldn't do much to him.

"I'm not going to sit by and let that fucker get away with this. I warned him to stay away from Kaden and he didn't listen. If you won't do something about it, then I will!" Luke practically yells at his brother.

I interject. "Luke, please don't go after him. He's fucking unhinged right now. He threatened to hurt you. Please, can we just take other measures? I'll pay more attention to my surroundings and park my car outside the front door of my office. I won't go anywhere alone. Please just don't go near him." He doesn't respond to my pleading, just listens, his arms still wrapped around me, as Jackson talks about speaking with his supervisor, and a possible restraining order.

Once he and Jackson seem to be done, Luke guides us to the bedroom. "Let's just take a breather and rest," he says while we undress and get in bed. "I'm sure you're exhausted from all this."

My brain is racing, but as Luke caresses my back and arm, I start to relax. Eventually, I fall asleep.

When I open my eyes again, it's dark outside the window of Luke's bedroom, and he's no longer in bed. Checking my phone, I see it's almost 6 a.m., and get up to look around the room, then I check the bathroom. Luke isn't in either. Heart pounding with anxiety, I rush out to the main area of the apartment. Still no Luke in sight.

Damn it, Luke!

Chapter Thirty-One

CONTROL IS AN ILLUSION

Luke

I'm currently attempting to restrain myself from marching right up to Tyler's front door. I don't want to approach him in front of his wife. She doesn't need to see what I'm about to do to him. She doesn't deserve that—not after whatever Tyler has probably put her through.

After Kaden fell asleep, I scoured the internet to find Tyler's full name. It took a little digging, but I finally found it. Thankfully, after calming my nerves and cuddling with Kaden for a bit, I was able to slip out from under him without waking him up. I know he would've stopped me from leaving, and I couldn't have that. I've been sitting outside Tyler's house for over an hour. Now, the sun is finally beginning to show itself. He should be up soon.

I'm taking the last sip of my coffee when I see his front door open. I watch him back his car out of the driveway and carefully follow him some distance behind, hoping he doesn't spot me. The drive to his office is about twenty minutes. As soon as we pull into the lot, I jump out and charge toward his car, barely giving him a chance to open his door before I rip him out of it.

"What the fu—" I don't let him finish his sentence as I throw the first punch. When I pin him to the car, he starts to struggle.

"What's the matter? You don't like being attacked in the parking lot of your office?" I throw another punch, and see blood trickle from his nose. This time Tyler swings back, connecting with my jaw. That just shatters any control I had on my anger.

I land a few more punches on his face before I have Tyler pinned to the ground by his throat. "I told you to stay the fuck away from him. You didn't fucking listen, did you?"

My hands are so tight around his throat he's starting to turn red. I'm so focused I don't hear someone coming up behind me, pulling me off Tyler.

"Luke, calm down. Stop, man. Don't do this."

How the fuck did Jackson get here?

Tyler is coughing, attempting to catch his breath while Jackson pulls me farther away from him, turning to put himself between us.

"Jackson, get out of my way!" I struggle with my brother, needing to finish what I came here for.

"Luke, stop." I freeze at the sound of Kaden's voice. His hands land firmly on the back of my hips. "Please. Just walk away with me."

My heart and mind are fighting with each other. Tyler needs to be stopped. I won't let him continue to hurt Kaden and get away with it, but I also don't want Kaden here to watch any of this.

Tyler staggers to his feet, clasping his neck while attempting to breathe properly again. "Fucking psychopath."

"Yeah, that's rich coming from you." Jackson faces Tyler. "You've been warned once before. For the last time, stay away from Kaden and Luke." They stare each other down until Tyler glances over my shoulder at Kaden.

"Don't even fucking look at him," I say, moving myself in front of Kaden to block his view.

"Walk away." Jackson gives one last instruction before Tyler gets back in his car and drives away.

Kaden walks around me and starts inspecting my face and hands. "Are you okay?"

"I'm fine. Would have been better if you'd let me finish what I came here to do."

"And what exactly is that, Luke? Because I don't want to have to explain to your aunts that you got arrested and need bail money—or worse."

"I don't know, Kaden, but he needs to be dealt with sooner rather than later. You think he's going to stop. This didn't sway him at all."

"And you think assaulting him is going to help our case at all when I bring this up to my supervisor?" Jackson's frustration spills into his voice. "I can't tell her this guy is stalking Kaden and skip the part where you beat the shit out of him."

"C'mon let's get out of here." Kaden nudges me toward the Jeep. "Thank you, Jackson, for helping. I'll take it from here."

"Leave him alone, Luke. I'll figure it out." Jackson's demand falls flat as we walk away.

"I drove my car, but I don't want to leave it here. Can I trust you to go straight home if I follow you?" Kaden's question is valid.

"He's not going to stop." I meet Kaden's eyes.

"Jackson is going to take care of it. Let's just wait for him to do what he can."

I stare into those pretty blue eyes that captured my attention the moment we saw each other. I can't purposely lie to him. I give the only answer I can with full transparency. "If he comes near you again, I won't let you stop me."

The look on his face tells me he knows it's the truth. "Go straight home, Luke. I'm following you."

Kissing him before we leave, our lips linger a little longer to savor the feeling. I don't know what Jackson has planned, but it had better happen fast. I don't trust Tyler to listen to any warnings at this point.

Attempting to get supply orders placed at the restaurant turns out to be harder than usual. My thoughts repeatedly spiral back to Tyler. I've texted and called Kaden a dozen times since we both left for work after this morning's incident. The last few responses have been reduced to one-word answers. No matter what, though, I won't apologize for worrying about him—whether he thinks it's extreme or not. After all those messages Tyler sent to Kaden, threatening both of us, he got what he deserved.

"Buddy, I can feel the anger radiating off you. Chill out until Jackson has a chance to do something about him. Kelsey knows to be on alert at the office. He's safe there." Gabe's words do nothing to lessen my unease about leaving Kaden unguarded.

Checking my watch, I see it's getting late in the afternoon. "I'm going to head out soon to meet him before he leaves the office."

My best friend nods as he throws an arm over my shoulders for a side-hug. "Do what you need to do. Call me if you need backup—for anything."

I'm putting my paperwork away when the pinging of messages sends me back on alert.

> Hey Bug. I'm heading home early. My last appointment cancelled.

I'm in the car already. Almost home, so stop worrying. I love you. See you soon.

I swear he's determined to kill me.

I'll be there in less than 30 minutes.

I gather my belongings and say goodnight to Gabe and the staff. When I get on the road, I call Kaden, but there's no answer. Accelerating, I barely pay attention to my surroundings, almost blind with anxiety. My calls keep going unanswered.

Halfway there, my speakers ring with an incoming call. "Kaden?"

"No, it's me. Where are you?" Jackson's tone sends my mind spinning as my heart rate skyrockets.

"I'm on my way to Kaden's. Tell me what's happening, Jackson."

"I'm on my way there, too. Kaden's in trouble, Luke. How far are you?"

Jackson's words fade out, my pounding heartbeats and the whooshing of blood in my ears overwhelming my senses.

Chapter Thirty-Two

I Mistakenly Threw Caution to the Wind

Kaden

A hand covers my mouth, and I'm thrust forward into my apartment as I unlock the door. I struggle but can't get free.

"Surprise. You should really pay more attention to your surroundings, Kaden. Your guard dogs can't be here 24/7." Tyler's voice is dripping with anger and amusement all at once.

"Did you think I would give up so easily? Your boyfriend doesn't scare me."

He walks us toward the living room, keeping his hand over my mouth, his other arm on my chest holding me against him. With as much strength as I can in this position, I throw my elbow back into his stomach. It's not much, but it throws him off balance enough for me to break his grip.

Tyler stands in the path to the front door with a smirk, blocking any chance of escape.

"Tyler, you have to stop. I don't understand why you're doing this. You left me. You didn't want me."

"Whether I wanted you or not, I couldn't have you. My father wouldn't have let us happen. He made it very clear when he found out about us."

Tyler's words start to make sense for a change. Since the day we became friends, he always said his father controlled everything he did—even choosing his career path.

"He doesn't get to have you, Kaden. I won't let him."

"Tyler, please just go home to your wife. This needs to end here."

"Marissa said the same thing when she found out about us this morning. It's over."

The thought of his wife ending their marriage scares me as much as Tyler does right now. Having no reason to stop pursuing me, he'll be more unpredictable than we thought.

Tyler's eyes fill with determination as he charges at me, grabbing my arms. "C'mon we're leaving."

Knowing I can't let him take me somewhere else, I swing at him, my fist connecting with his cheekbone. His eyes burn with rage as he recovers and grabs me by my throat, holding me at arm's length. Tyler is squeezing hard enough to block my airway, and panicked, I swing my fist at him but can't quite reach him. I kick my leg up then, thankfully hitting him directly in the balls. Tyler hunches over, letting go of my throat, but quickly recovers, punching me in the face. I instantly taste blood in the back of my throat as I stumble backward, falling to the floor. On the way down, my head smashes into the corner of the end table next to the couch.

Everything turns fuzzy, and I can't make out the sudden loud noises in the room. I touch my temple, cringing at the pain, and feel something wet on my skin. That's when my hearing is finally able to focus on what I realize is *screaming* in the room.

"Luke, stop. I've got him. Go help Kaden." I can't tell whose voice that was, but I heard Luke's name, and then the sudden warmth of his skin is on me.

"Fuck, you're bleeding." I hear Luke's voice over the yelling in the background.

"Luke?"

"I'm here. Just relax—everything is going to be okay now." Luke sits on the floor and lifts my head and shoulders enough to rest on his lap.

I'm able to open my eyes and focus on those green soul-stealers once again. Except this time, they're laced with agony.

"Hi, Bug."

"Hi, Angel." That soft smile of his melts me every time. "I was so worried about you. The thought of losing you..." Luke clenches his eyes shut. "Losing you would break me, Kaden."

"You aren't going to lose me. You're stuck with me, babe." I give him a faint chuckle.

"Being stuck with someone has never sounded so good."

"I'm sorry I wasn't more caref—" I get cut off by shouting behind us.

"Jackson, get him the fuck out of here," Luke yells across the room, to where I see Tyler, his face pressed against the wall, Jackson detaining him in cuffs. Tyler is shouting at a woman standing behind Jackson. It takes me a second to realize it's his wife.

What is she doing here?

Dakota comes rushing into the apartment with another officer in uniform just as Jackson is walking Tyler toward the door.

"Guys, take him out of here. I need to stay with Luke and Kaden." Jackson hands Tyler over to the officer.

Marissa walks over to Luke and me from the kitchen, while Jackson fills the officers in. "Here's a wet cloth to wipe up some of the blood." She cautiously hands it to Luke.

"How did you all wind up here?" Confused how this all transpired, I ask and stare at Marissa.

"I've known of you for a while, Kaden. I just didn't know why or how much Tyler was obsessing over you until recently." Marissa's words leave me even more confused.

"I think you need to hear what she has to say, Kaden." Jackson joins us when the others leave.

Marissa moves to the chair next to us while Luke helps me sit up on the couch.

"We got married less than six months from the day he proposed. Both our families pushed us to not have a long engagement, since we've all known each other forever. A couple months after the wedding, I saw Tyler looking at one of your profiles on social media. I didn't think anything of it." Marissa's expression is solemn, something uneasy blooming in her gaze.

"Over the next few months, I noticed him watching you on different platforms more than a few times. I finally asked him who you were. He had never caught me before, so when I made it known that I'd noticed, he didn't take it well. I got accused of snooping, and was told you were just a friend from college. So, I let it go. I didn't think anything further about it—until the night we saw you at Luke's restaurant." She looks down at her hands, fiddling with her cuticles. "It was a spur-of-the-moment dinner. We'd been arguing a lot lately in the months before that night, so I thought he was just trying to be nice and spend time with me. When we passed your table, I noticed you, and the look on your face when you saw him. When he followed you to the bathroom, I was afraid to go see what was going on. I knew he would be mad." Marissa pauses, taking a few deep breaths.

"Did he hurt you, Marissa?" I have to know.

"Let's just say he's a scary man when he's angry, but I have a feeling you were already aware of that a long time ago."

I nod, reaching out and taking her hand in mine.

"When Luke walked you out of the restaurant, I knew there was more to what was going on between you two. I never mentioned it to Tyler, though. I started searching his office for anything I could find when he wasn't home. I watched your social media posts, and noticed every time you made plans to go somewhere, suddenly Tyler had plans with his friends."

"A couple weeks ago, I followed him out and saw him go into that big bar, The Garden. I didn't go in, being too afraid he would see me. But when I saw you and Luke come out a little while later, he followed you out." Marissa's cheeks turn red.

Mine mimic hers, already knowing what she saw.

"I saw him watching you both. I think that's when it really hit me. I knew this wasn't just old friends who'd had a spat or something. Then I followed him again yesterday afternoon after I saw him furiously typing on a phone that wasn't his. It was one of those pay-per-use burner phones. I saw what happened outside your office. I was dialing the police when your friend came up and stopped Tyler."

"I followed you home, sorry." She half-laughs at her apology. I smile in return. "I saw Jackson running into the building a few minutes after you. With him looking so much like Luke, I figured he knew something was going on as well."

"When Tyler came home all banged up this morning, I confronted him. Told him I knew everything, and he needed to stop what he was doing. He turned volatile, telling me it's over and he'd never wanted me anyway. He started packing his bags, so I figured he was just leaving, until I heard him mumbling to himself. It was about you."

Marissa looks behind her at Jackson as he nods to her. "I didn't know your name, so I started scouring the internet for them." She looks from one brother to the other. "I went to the restaurant's website and found Luke. Then I found Jackson by making the connections between the restaurant's name, Luke's profile, and then their shared last name. I was going to go to Luke first, but when I saw Jackson was a cop, I went to the precinct looking for him. Told them everything that I witnessed over the past year."

"Micah reached out to me to verify what Marissa said about yesterday." Jackson turns to me. "I was near the precinct, so I went to meet up with them. I called you as soon as we left the precinct to come here. When you didn't answer, I called Luke."

My mind is still attempting to process everything Marissa told us. "So, he's been following me for how long? Since you got married?"

"Honestly, Kaden, I think it was way before that. Probably since you guys graduated. He was always guarded when looking at his phone or talking about any of his friends during dental school. It seemed he was content watching you from afar—until Luke came into your life."

Luke grips onto me from behind. "He mentioned something in the text messages about the party where Luke and I met. He must have followed me there."

"He was probably watching us all night." Luke's thinking the same thing as I am.

"I can't believe I was that oblivious."

"Kaden, you couldn't have known he was following you." Marissa shakes her head. "He obviously did a good job at hiding it from all of us."

"This isn't on you." Luke kisses my temple, pulling me into his arms. "Don't let him make you feel any worse about yourself than he already has."

"Jackson, what happens to him now?" Luke asks the question that was on the tip of my tongue.

"I don't know exactly, but I'm sure he'll be charged with assault and restraining Kaden. And with all that Marissa witnessed and our corroboration, I think stalking will be on that list, too. As for him going to jail for more than a couple months, it depends on the judge—whether he considers the other offenses and the degree of the assault. Tyler strangling Kaden doesn't help his situation."

"So, he may essentially get a slap on the wrist?" Marissa is the concerned one now.

Jackson doesn't respond, all of us already knowing the answer.

The silence is deafening.

Chapter Thirty-Three

SAY IT WITH ME – "I AM ENOUGH"

Two Months Later

Kaden

I can't resist staring at Luke as he gets dressed to go out tonight. How did I get so lucky?

"If you keep undressing me with your eyes before I'm even fully dressed, we'll never get out the door."

Guilty.

"I can't help it if you turn me on. Maybe you should get dressed in the bathroom, or we're going to be late." At least I can be honest with him.

I receive a headshake of disbelief and a chuckle. "That sounds like a problem you need to deal with on your own." I smile at his typical response to my flirting. He's grown more accustomed to my bratty behavior. I'm happy to report that my little punishments have only gotten better.

The past couple months have been a whirlwind of speaking with investigators as they've attempted to find out everything they can about Tyler and his actions over the past year. He wound up pleading guilty to all the charges in exchange for a lesser sentence, knowing that evidence Marissa had on him—after finding both burner phones he was using and the text messages he'd sent me—would be damning to his case. She also found some videos on his personal phone, taken when he was following me. There were more than a dozen from the past year, including the night I met Luke. Knowing he was there, watching us from the next stall, has made me more anxious and aware that I need to take notice of my surroundings when I'm out in public.

Tyler got less than a year, which is still more than we'd thought he would get. Any punishment is better than none, I suppose. All I want now is for him to reflect on what he did to me. I can only hope it'll be enough time that he won't try to repeat any of this once he gets out.

"Alright, let's go before Fred realizes we're leaving and guilt trips you into staying home." Luke rushes me out the door before we get yelled at by our friends for being late once again. It's become a normal occurrence for us, but we're trying to break the cycle.

When we arrive only a couple minutes late, our smartass friends give us a standing ovation, whistling and all. All eyes are suddenly on us, and I could crawl into a hole. Thankfully, Luke pulls me into him, and safe in his arms I forget all about my embarrassment.

"Alright assholes, you can stop with the theatrics now." Luke's scolding is all in fun, provoking a round of laughter.

"Awww, someone's grumpy. I guess that means they'll be sneaking around later."

Gabe has called us out a couple times now for sneaking off for 'alone' time during our outings. We aren't exactly inconspicuous about it, but we really don't care. We enjoy our trysts in random bathrooms or parking lots, in or out of a vehicle. We haven't exactly gotten caught yet, so until then, we'll have our fun.

We all fall into our usual chatter—or debates, because of course we can't go one night without Gabe and Connor disagreeing on something. I think Connor is just a little jealous about Gabe taking up so much of Ender's time lately. Not like he's one to talk, but I'm not getting involved in all their business.

Faith is back to ignoring Dakota tonight, which is another chaotic situation I've stopped trying to understand. Poor guy has been through the wringer with her the past couple months, but he hasn't given up on her yet, so I'll give him an A+ for effort.

"Hey everyone, sorry we're late." Kelsey and Austin have become a part of our family here since that first night, and then Austin saving me from Tyler. They fit in with us seamlessly. What's more, their arrival has ended Gabe and Connor's bickering—for now.

"Anyone need another beer?" Austin asks before heading off.

"I'll come with you." Luke and Austin have become close. I can't count how many times Luke has thanked him for stepping in to help me.

Lanie comes to sit next to me. "Having fun, butthead?"

"Always. What's going on with you and Jackson? Haven't heard from you much the past couple weeks."

"I just saw you last night at dinner and game night, Kaden."

"That's different. The parental units were around. We can't talk about anything private around them. You know they can't keep a secret to save their lives."

"Truth." She hesitates sharing whatever is going on. "We're good. Just some things you and I should talk about. Jackson says it'll be good for me to talk to you about it, so I'm trying."

"Lanie, I don't like the way that sounds."

"It's fine, I promise. We can talk tomorrow. I'll come over for takeout and a movie."

"I'm holding you to your word." I give her a steely look to make sure she knows I won't let her back out of it at the last minute.

"I'll be there." She reassures me with a side-hug and kiss on the cheek.

"Hey, did I say I was sharing her tonight?" Jackson reaches out, taking Lanie's hand and pulling her toward an area where people are dancing.

"She was mine first!" I yell at him as they walk away, all of us falling into laughter.

I walk to the bar in search of the man whose presence I've grown to crave being in. "Are you going to hog my man all night, Austin?"

"It's the least you can give me, since I saved your life." Austin's running joke for stealing Luke's time away from me never misses its mark.

"Okay, okay, we can share him tonight."

"Wait, who's sharing who, now?" Bryce has once again overheard our conversation. I swear the guy has supersonic hearing, like a dolphin or something.

"No one is sharing anyone, at least when it comes to Kaden and me." Luke pulls me in front of him, possessively wrapping his arms around my waist.

"That's a disappointment, but I get it. I wouldn't want to share you two, either." Bryce walks away with a wink and a smirk. He's become a regular staple in our nights here, often flirting with me just to get a rise out of Luke. If Luke didn't already know he was doing it to tease him, we probably would have been banned from the bar by now.

"On that note, I'm going to join the others, and you two can go do your thing. It's about that time isn't it?" Luke gives Austin the finger as he walks away, cackling at himself.

"Are we really that bad?" I ask Luke, leaning back into him.

"Yes. Your favorite thing in the world is getting me hard in public—or have you forgotten?"

"Second favorite."

"Oh yeah, what's the first?" he whispers, his lips brushing my ear.

"You punishing me for making you hard in public." I reach behind me, palming him, already feeling him begin to swell. I can't help the silent laugh that escapes me at how easy he is to tease.

"That's funny—it happens to be my favorite thing too." He bites my earlobe, and I know it's time to go.

I take his hand and lead him out the door without any objections on his part. His surprised expression when I open the driver's side door, nudging him to get inside, makes me want to drag him into the back seat right here and now.

"Ummm are we going somewhere?" he asks when I get in.

"Take me home, Luke." He stares at me for a moment before starting the engine.

The ride home feels longer than it usually does. I guess that could be because we didn't get up to our typical escapades before leaving.

I lead Luke into his building and straight to his bedroom once in his apartment. Fred protests when I close the bedroom door behind us—you'd think he'd be used to it by now.

"Angel, what do you have up your sleeve?"

"Besides giving you complete control over my body tonight?" I pause, squeezing his hips as I pull him closer. "Keeping you for the rest of my life." It comes out as a whisper.

The heat in his eyes turns soft before he gently pulls my lips to his.

He walks me backward toward the bed, until the backs of my knees hit the edge. I take a seat while I work on unbuckling his belt and lowering his jeans to his thighs. Luke caresses my hair as I press my face into the crease of his groin, inhaling deeply, letting the musky smell of him consume me for a moment. Then I run my tongue over his skin before giving his beautiful cock the attention it deserves.

The way he's gazing down at me, full of affection, does that tsunami thing to my stomach again—just like the night we met.

"I'll never get tired of this view, Angel."

I pull off him with a smile. "I can't say I mind the view myself." I continue undressing him, his lustful eyes not leaving mine.

"You need to stop looking at me like that before I spoil whatever you have planned here."

I push him back and stand to undress myself. Luke brushes his hands all over my body as I remove each piece of clothing, his touch sending goosebumps to places his hands haven't been, yet. I throw my arms around his neck, pressing my lips softly to his as his fingers seek my hole. I see and feel the moment he finds my surprise instead.

"Baby, did you wear a present for me?" He grins, firmly tapping on the plug I've been wearing all night for him, causing me to gasp against his lips.

"I have no idea what you're talking about." I bat my eyelashes at him sweetly.

"Show me." The gravel in his voice tells me it's not a request.

I turn and kneel on the bed, elbows on the mattress, my legs spread as far as they can go in this position. I feel his hands spread me open and hear his sharp intake of breath when he sees the pretty green jewel on the base of the plug.

"Do you like it?" I ask him over my shoulder.

Luke just nods, not taking his eyes off it. "Why green?"

"It's been my favorite color since the day we met." He blesses me with that iceberg-melter of a smile again.

Luke pulls on the base, pumping it slowly when the movement pulls a gasp out of me.

"As pretty as it is, I'm extremely jealous of it right now." he admits as he pulls it fully out and throws it on the bed. I'm taken by surprise when he replaces it with his tongue. He's been taking things slow, exploring what he's into, and until now, rimming me isn't something he's tried. It doesn't take long to find out just how much he's enjoying himself.

Luke buries his face in me, sucking and licking like a starving man. One hand finds my cock, stroking firmly while his tongue plunges in and out of me. The sensation is pure euphoria, unlike anything else, and I'm helpless to control the moans and hissed profanities that escape my mouth, Luke is *good* at this.

He pauses, briefly between each taste of my hole. "Damn you taste so good." Lick. "I see why you enjoy doing this." Suck. "I could come just from this." His tongue then dives as deep as it can go it has my entire body trembling with pleasure.

"Fuck, you're killing me, babe." The words come out sounding more like whimpers.

Instead of continuing, his face leaves my body, and I regret saying anything. He wastes no time grabbing the lube from the nightstand drawer, then returns to his position behind me.

Luke rubs his hand along my spine, gently pushing me down into the mattress. I feel the cold gel on his fingers when he briefly enters me to slick me up. Then he replaces his fingers with his cock, bending his body entirely over mine until we're skin to skin. The slow drives into me, combined with the sensual way his hands massage my hips and stomach, have me grabbing Luke by the hair, pulling his head forward until I can suffocate him with a kiss that would make the Devil jealous.

When we come up for air, Luke's words cement my resolve to keep him forever. "I didn't know how much I needed you until you found me, and I'm going to make sure you know your worth every day for the rest of our lives." He continues slowly thrusting into me while the muscle in my chest pleads with me to break out of its cage, desperate to wrap itself around Luke, protecting him at all costs. "Thank you for loving me, Angel."

Once again, this man shakes me to my core. "Luke, I need you to get up." He obeys my breathless instruction without question, and I turn him to lie on his back. Then I straddle him, seating myself on his cock.

"I need to look you in the eyes when I say this." I cup his face in my hands as I leisurely roll my hips. My lips caress his, moved by the truest words they've ever spoken. "You are lovable, you are loved, you are enough. If I have to spend the rest of our lives telling you every single day to make you believe it, I will." I barely see his eyes water before his fingers tangle in my hair and he pulls me firmly into him.

Kissing his neck and shoulders as far as I can reach, I feel his body trembling under my lips. His arm is like a vise around me, and I couldn't move even if I wanted to. The embrace seems to last an eternity and yet not long enough.

When he slowly releases me, the tears smeared across his face shatter my heart to pieces. "I love you, Bug." I lean in, swiping up his tears with my lips.

"I love you, Kaden." Our kiss starts off gentle as he begins thrusting up into me, picking up pace the more frantically our tongues and mouths connect with each other. At last, he flips me over, leaning back on his knees and pushing my knees to my chest, where I spread and hold them for him.

Luke fists my cock, stroking in pace with the pounding he's giving my hole. "Fuck, I'm coming." I barely get the words out before my cum is spurting onto my stomach, Luke's hand squeezing every last drop out of me.

Luke groans, long and guttural as he slams into me one final time, the warmth of his cum filling me.

As he regains his wits, heavy breaths surrounding us, his hand from around my cock scoops up more of my cum. Luke pushes my mouth open, his cum-covered fingers circling around my tongue. The blissfulness coursing through my body only heightens when he leans down, licking up the rest of my cum before bringing his mouth to mine in a heated kiss. His tongue massages mine, and I swallow desperately, wanting—*needing*—to consume all that is Luke.

Luke's dick is back inside me, because he just *had* to feel me on him for a little while longer.

He stays right where he is, our bodies pressed firmly against each other. Connected. Content just to stay like this for now.

"Did you really expect to meet someone at that party we went to?" Luke's question startles me as it breaks the silence.

"No. Not at all. I only went to hang out with Faith and Lanie. I knew Lanie wouldn't let me stay home even if I tried." He chuckles, knowing exactly what I mean. "Did you?"

"I was definitely not there to find anyone. I only went to appease Jackson and Dakota."

"I guess we have them to thank then, huh?" I smile, thinking of how much I owe Lanie for helping me find my lobster.

"Yeah, I need to thank Lanie for making that shirt, or I would have never known you were her brother." His laughter still gives me warm flutters.

"You mean 'Just the Brother,'" I clarify, reminding him of some of the first words he ever said to me.

Lifting his head from my shoulder, eyes focused on mine, his words extract all the air from my lungs. "You're not '*Just*' anything, Kaden. '*Just*' is not enough to describe anything about you. '*Just*' will *never* be enough."

Thank you, Goddesses.

Epilogue

FULL CIRCLE

Three Years Later

Luke

"Lanie looks gorgeous in that dress. Your circle did a great job helping her choose the right one." I take Kaden's hand as we head over to the reception area of the venue.

"I couldn't agree more," Connor boasts from where he's following behind us with Austin.

"I hope she feels as beautiful as she looks." Whenever Kaden speaks about his sister, his tone radiates love.

"If she didn't before Jackson saw her, I can guarantee he's making sure of it right now." My brother worships the ground that woman walks on. I think he has since the day they met.

Kaden squeezes my hand. His soft smile says that's exactly what's happening while they take their photos at the gazebo by the lake.

We all tend to the first task at hand—going to the bartender's station where Dakota, Gabe, and Ender are waiting for us, drinks already ordered.

"What happened, Dakota? Faith ditch you, again?" Connor, always poking the bear.

223

"Ha ha, very funny. I think she went with Kelsey to help Lanie. Apparently, it's a thing where the bridesmaids have to fix the bride's dress thing in the back, so it looks good in the pictures."

"It's called a train, you Neanderthal." Connor being Connor, again.

"Wait, who's running a train on who, now?" Bryce and that damn sense of humor of his.

"Are you ever not thinking about sex, Bryce?" Austin asks the question that's on all of our minds, and Bryce grins at our laughter.

"Why would I want to do that?" He huffs like it's the obvious answer. "Check in with you guys in a little while. Have fun!"

The party gets underway, and our group seems to be the loudest. When the DJ comes over the mic, letting us know it's time for the bride and groom to make their grand entrance, we settle down, so the spotlight is on them.

The thunderous applause and cheering when they enter the room overpowers the music they chose for the entrance. The smiles on Lanie and Jackson's faces are like none I've ever seen. My Angel's smile is breathtaking, of course, but the newlyweds' are a different version of happy. I look at Kaden, wondering if his smile could get any better if it was us making that grand entrance.

"What are you staring at, Bug?"

"Perfection."

Kaden's always shaking his head at me. "No one is perfect, Luke. That pedestal you put me on is going to collapse one day."

I lean into him, wrapping my arm around his waist. "Then I guess I'll just have to keep rebuilding it, won't I?" My favorite shade of pink covers his cheek as I kiss it.

As I watch their first dance, I know it will forever be a core memory of seeing my brother in one of the happiest moments of his life. Every time he looks at Lanie, I can see the evidence all over his face.

It's not long before our chosen family regroups for celebratory shots all around.

"To a night of laughing, dancing, and maybe a little smashing." Faith, Lanie, and Kaden burst into laughter while the rest of us exchange confused looks until Lanie finishes her toast. "But Luke and Kaden aren't allowed to leave early!"

The running joke has never gotten old, which is probably our fault for continuing our little trysts. Kaden's cock-teasing has only escalated over the years, but I'm not complaining.

"We promise to not disappear tonight." As I give my word to Lanie, hoping I can keep it, Kaden's hand palms my ass. I stifle the laugh that almost breaks free, turning my head toward Kaden to see his devilish grin.

"Jesus Christ, you two, do you ever stop giving each other fuck-me eyes?" Faith's comment comes out sounding more like amazement than a complaint.

"I can't help it if weddings make me want to get down on one knee, too." Kaden's eyes pop open wide at my comment.

"Oh no you don't, fucker. Don't you dare propose to my brother at my wedding. He deserves his own special moment." Lanie gets all up in my face pointing a finger at me, taking me more seriously than I meant.

"You're right, Lanie. He does, and so do you. I would never take either of your special moments away. Today is about you and Jackson. And I couldn't be happier to call you my sister." I wrap Lanie in my arms as her eyes fill with emotion. Kissing her temple, I lean close to her ear. "Thank you for taking such good care of Jackson for me. You're an amazing woman. Don't ever forget that."

At that, Lanie gently pushes me away. "Stop that right now, before you ruin my makeup." She runs into Jackson's arms, hiding herself from me. Everyone's laughter fades as we disperse, Kaden and I making our way to the dance floor.

Surprisingly, Kaden behaves himself—mostly. Lanie and Jackson join us on the dance floor after making their rounds with the guests, right before Lanie's requested song comes on. When she and Kaden both turn around, shoving their asses in Jackson's and my groins, I know I'm done for. It doesn't take long for my cock to get painfully hard.

"Okay, we're done here." I grab Kaden by the waist and drag him off the dance floor.

"Don't you fuck my brother at my wedding! You promised!" Lanie screams after us, making everyone within earshot stare in shock.

"You didn't play fair. Deal's off!" I yell back at her as Kaden plays innocent.

"Why, Bug, whatever do you mean?"

"Yeah, yeah, get in there," I tell him, nudging him into the first bathroom we find.

"Now, Bug, you aren't suggesting I did anything on purpose out there, are you?"

I back him into the wall, trapping him with my body against his.

"Not at all, Angel. You're an innocent bystander. I would never accuse you of something like that, would I?"

"I'm glad we see eye-to-eye on this, then."

"Me, too." I take Kaden's hand, forming it into a fist and place it in his mouth. "Now be a *Good Boy* and take your punishment."

I recreate the scene from our first night, reversing our roles. Down on my knees in front of Kaden, I take his cock out of his slacks and suck him hard and fast as he gives my throat a pounding like no other. I've come to agree with him when he said the view from down here is just as good as from above. According to Kaden, I've reached expert level at sucking his dick, and I won't argue if it gives me the chance to do it as often as I please.

Kaden's hand from his mouth joins his other hand wrapped up in my hair, thrusting himself as far as he can go, holding me still as his cum shoots down my throat.

"Fuuuuccccckkkk." His moaning expletive comes out far louder than I think he meant it to.

When he's as empty as he can possibly be, I rise from my knees. "Angel, I don't think you know how to listen very well. Anyone walking by, definitely heard you enjoying yourself. I guess I'll have to find a better way to punish you, then maybe you'll learn your lesson."

"It's cute you think that's a punishment."

He never ceases to make me laugh. I must be the luckiest man alive to have won Kaden's heart. Growing old has never sounded better than with him by my side.

"I love you, Kaden."

"I love you, Luke."

Acknowledgments

I cannot say thank you enough for the amazing support I have received from friends, family, my teams, and fellow authors throughout this process. It's been a crazy ride!

First, my friends and family. You have listened to me incessantly talking about Luke and Kaden, along with the rest of the gang, for months on end without once telling me to STFU! Patience doesn't come close to what I would call it. I love you all, but don't expect it to stop. We have five more books to go...in this series.

To the few fellow authors that guided me on all things related to self-publishing, finding artists for cover and illustration designs, and forming ARC and Street teams. Thank you for not making me feel like a nuisance during your busy lives and writing your own WIP. You all know who you are!

To my original ARC team for JINE, you're amazing! I am so glad I had the opportunity to meet you all and chat on a daily basis, whether you wrote a review or not! Our group chat has some of the most amusing and craziest conversations I've ever had. Don't forget, "It's always best to not ask what one walks in on."

What can I say about my ARC and Street Teams as one unit? You're all as much as a chaotic hot mess as I am and I love every moment we spend wreaking havoc in our group chat. Even though I seem like a madwoman to strangers in a random coffee shop, laughing hysterically at our banter, every day I still look forward to seeing another "On Today's Episode of Haleigh's Chaotic Hype Crew" update graphic. IYKYK <3

A special thank you to the most positive person I've ever met—always finding the sunshine even through the darkest clouds in our lives—Travis. Words could never express how much your friendship means to me. You've unwaveringly supported me every step of the way through this journey. I was truly blessed when you came into my life. I love you!

To my ride or dies, my coven, my biggest supporters, my "stop getting in your fucking head" besties, my cheerleaders without the pom poms and skirts (I may have to buy some pom poms for book two), that make up my Alpha team. You have all been with me since day one. You never faltered for one minute in your support. You told me to stop my shit when I was overthinking everything! Instead of sugar-coating, you were all brutally honest about every word I wrote that just didn't sound right. I could not have done this without all of you. <u>Our</u> baby is out in the world for all to read.

Thank you. I love you!
Valeska F.
Laura D.
Danielle S.

Mom, I love and miss you every single day.
You aren't here to see this, but I did it. <3

For my readers

Thank you for taking the time to get to know my guys. I hope you enjoyed Luke and Kaden's love story as much as I have creating it. They hold a special place in my heart for many reasons. While they are amazing men and their love has no boundaries, they are only the beginning of this journey. I hope you join us to see what the rest of the gang has in store for you.

And if you think that knowing Jackson and Lanie getting their HEA means there isn't a story to tell, you're sadly mistaken. We all knew they were a love-at-first-sight couple. Their story isn't just about falling in love, but you'll have to stick around for Book five if you want to know more. <3

Next up, Ender and Gabe's turn at finding love! My sweet broken boy's story may tear your heart to pieces, but I promise to put it back together again. Bring a box of tissues with you.

You've been warned!

Finally, to my younger self...
I finished the unfinished story.

About the Author

I'm a weirdo at heart. I loved writing short stories as a teenager and rarely let anyone read them. I still have some of them in a box in the garage. I grew up in the Northeast and have slowly migrated south over the years where I live with family and friends.

Luke and Kaden's story began in one of my dreams not too long ago, throwing me right into this world of characters I have fallen in love with. Each of them have their own unique story. I'm so excited to put them to paper and share them with the world.

Connect with Haleigh

Join Haleigh Falcon's Socials Club Facebook group for advance sneak peeks on The Charlotte Socials, new project announcements, and there's always a little fun happening!

Subscribe to my monthly newsletter to stay up to date on signing events, upcoming promotions, and much more!

Find my social media accounts on Linktree
https://linktr.ee/haleighfalconauthor

www.ingramcontent.com/pod-product-compliance
Lightning Source LLC
Chambersburg PA
CBHW07074S180626
46818CB00007B/2990